Kate Douglas Smith Wiggin

Timothy's quest : a story for anybody, young or old, who cares to read it

Kate Douglas Smith Wiggin

Timothy's quest : a story for anybody, young or old, who cares to read it

ISBN/EAN: 9783337056971

Printed in Europe, USA, Canada, Australia, Japan

Cover: Foto ©Andreas Hilbeck / pixelio.de

More available books at **www.hansebooks.com**

TIMOTHY'S QUEST

A STORY FOR ANYBODY, YOUNG OR OLD,
WHO CARES TO READ IT

BY

KATE DOUGLAS WIGGIN

AUTHOR OF " BIRDS' CHRISTMAS CAROL," " THE STORY OF PATSY,"
" A SUMMER IN A CAÑON," ETC.

BOSTON AND NEW YORK
HOUGHTON, MIFFLIN AND COMPANY
The Riverside Press, Cambridge
1892

TWENTY-THIRD THOUSAND.

The Riverside Press, Cambridge, Mass., U. S. A.
Electrotyped and Printed by H. O. Houghton & Company.

To

NORA

DEAREST SISTER, STERNEST CRITIC,

BEST FRIEND.

CONTENTS.

SCENE XV.

SCENE XVI.

TIMOTHY'S QUEST.

SCENE I.

Number Three, Minerva Court. First floor front.

FLOSSY MORRISON LEARNS THE SECRET OF DEATH WITHOUT EVER HAVING LEARNED THE SECRET OF LIFE.

MINERVA COURT! Veil thy face, O Goddess of Wisdom, for never, surely, was thy fair name so ill bestowed as when it was applied to this most dreary place!

It was a little less than street, a little more than alley, and its only possible claim to decency came from comparison with the busier thoroughfare out of which it opened. This was so much fouler, with its dirt and noise, its stands of refuse fruit and vegetables, its dingy shops and all the miserable traffic that the place engendered, its rickety doorways blocked with lounging men, its

Blowsabellas leaning on the window-sills, that the Court seemed by contrast a most desirable and retired place of residence.

But it was a dismal spot, nevertheless, with not even an air of faded gentility to recommend it. It seemed to have no better days behind it, nor to hold within itself the possibility of any future improvement. It was narrow, and extended only the length of a city block, yet it was by no means wanting in many of those luxuries which mark this era of modern civilization. There were groceries, with commodious sample-rooms attached, at each corner, and a small saloon, called " The Dearest Spot " (which it undoubtedly was in more senses than one), in the basement of a house at the farther end. It was necessary, however, for the bibulous native who dwelt in the middle of the block to waste some valuable minutes in dragging himself to one of these fountains of bliss at either end; but at the time my story opens a wide-awake philanthropist was fitting up a neat and attractive little bar-room, called " The Oasis," at a point equally distant between the other two springs of human joy.

This benefactor of humanity had a vaulting ambition. He desired to slake the thirst of every man in Christendom; but this being impossible from the very nature of things, he determined to settle in some arid spot like Minerva Court, and irrigate it so sweetly and copiously that all men's noses would blossom as the roses. To supply his brothers' wants, and create new ones at the same time, was his purpose in establishing this Oasis in the Desert of Minerva Court; and it might as well be stated here that he was prospered in his undertaking, as any man is sure to be who cherishes lofty ideals and attends to his business industriously.

The Minerva Courtier thus had good reason to hope that the supply of liquid refreshment would bear some relation to the demand; and that the march of modern progress would continue to diminish the distance between his own mouth and that of the bottle, which, as he took it, was the be-all and end-all of existence.

At present, however, as the Oasis was not open to the public, children carrying pitchers of beer were often to be seen hurrying to and fro on their miserable errands. But there were very few children in Minerva Court, thank God! — they were not popular there. There were frowzy, sleepy-

looking women hanging out of their win
dows, gossiping with their equally unkempt
and haggard neighbors; apathetic men sitting on the doorsteps, in their shirt-sleeves,
smoking; a dull, dirty baby or two sport-
ing itself in the gutter; while the sound of
a melancholy accordion (the chosen instrument of poverty and misery) floated from
an upper chamber, and added its discordant
mite to the general desolation.

The sidewalks had apparently never known
the touch of a broom, and the middle of the
street looked more like an elongated junk-
heap than anything else. Every smell known
to the nostrils of man was abroad in the
air, and several were floating about waiting
modestly to be classified, after which they
intended to come to the front and outdo the
others if they could.

That was Minerva Court! A little piece
of your world, my world, God's world (and
the Devil's), lying peacefully fallow, awaiting the services of some inspired Home Missionary Society.

In a front room of Number Three, a dilap-
idated house next the corner, there lay a
still, white shape, with two women watching
by it.

A sheet covered it. Candles burned at the head, striving to throw a gleam of light on a dead face that for many a year had never been illuminated from within by the brightness of self-forgetting love or kindly sympathy. If you had raised the sheet, you would have seen no happy smile as of a half-remembered, innocent childhood; the smile — is it of peaceful memory or serene anticipation? — that sometimes shines on the faces of the dead.

Such life-secrets as were . exposed by Death, and written on that still countenance in characters that all might read, were painful ones. Flossy Morrison was dead. The name "Flossy" was a relic of what she termed her better days (Heaven save the mark!), for she had been called Mrs. Morrison of late years, — "Mrs. F. Morrison," who took "children to board, and no questions asked" — nor answered. She had lived forty-five years, as men reckon summers and winters; but she had never learned, in all that time, to know her Mother, Nature, her Father, God, nor her brothers and sisters, the children of the world. She had lived friendless and unfriendly, keeping none of the ten commandments, nor yet the eleventh, which is the greatest of all; and now there was no human being to slip a flower into the still hand, to kiss the clay-cold lips at the remembrance of some sweet word that had fallen from them, or drop a tear and say, " I loved her! "

Apparently, the two watchers did not regard Flossy Morrison even in the light of " the dear remains," as they are sometimes called at country funerals. They were in the best of spirits (there was an abundance of beer), and their gruesome task would be over in a few hours; for it was nearly four o'clock in the morning, and the body was to be taken away at ten.

" I tell you one thing, Ettie, Flossy has n't left any bother for her friends," remarked Mrs. Nancy Simmons, settling herself back in her rocking-chair. " As she did n't own anything but the clothes on her back, there won't be any quarreling over the property! " and she chuckled at her delicate humor.

" No," answered her companion, who, whatever her sponsors in baptism had christened her, called herself Ethel Montmorency. " I s'pose the furniture, poor as it is, will pay the funeral expenses; and if she 's got any debts, why, folks will have to whistle for their money, that 's all."

" The only thing that worries me is the children," said Mrs. Simmons.

" You must be hard up for something to worry about, to take those young ones on your mind. They ain't yours nor mine, and what's more, nobody knows who they do belong to, and nobody cares. Soon as breakfast's over we'll pack 'em off to some institution or other, and that'll be the end of it. What did Flossy say about 'em, when you spoke to her yesterday ? "

" I asked her what she wanted done with the young ones, and she said, ' Do what you like with 'em, drat 'em, — it don't make no odds to me ! ' and then she turned over and died. Those was the last words she spoke, dear soul ; but, Lor', she wasn't more 'n half sober, and hadn't been for a week."

" She was sober enough to keep her own counsel, I can tell you that," said the gentle Ethel. " I dón't believe there's a living soul that knows where those children came from ; — not that anybody cares, now that there ain't any money in 'em."

" Well, as for that, I only know that when Flossy was seeing better days and lived in the upper part of the city, she used to have money come every month for taking care of the boy. Where it come from I don't know; but I kind of surmise it was a long distance off. Then she took to drinking, and got lower and lower down until she came here, six months ago. I don't suppose the boy's folks, or whoever it was sent the money, knew the way she was living, though they could n't have cared much, for they never came to see how things were; and he was in an asylum before Flossy took him, I found that out; but, anyhow, the money stopped coming three months ago. Flossy wrote twice to the folks, whoever they were, but did n't get no answer to her letters; and she told me that she should turn the boy out in a week or two if some cash did n't turn up in that time. She would n't have kept him so long as this if he had n't been so handy taking care of the baby."

"Well, who does the baby belong to?"

"You ask me too much," replied Nancy, taking another deep draught from the pitcher. "Help yourself, Ettie; there's plenty more where that came from. Flossy never liked the boy, and always wanted to get rid of him, but could n't afford to. He's a dreadful queer, old-fashioned little kid, and so smart that he's gettin' to be a reg'lar nuisance round the house. But you see he and the baby, — Gabrielle 's her name, but they call her Lady Gay, or some such trash, after that actress that comes here so much, — well, they are so in love with one another that wild horses could n't drag 'em apart; and I think Flossy had a kind of a likin' for Gay, as much as she ever had for anything. I guess she never abused either of 'em; she was too careless for that. And so — what was I talkin' about? Oh, yes. Well, I don't know who the baby is, nor who paid for her keep; but she 's goin' to be one o' your high-steppers, and no mistake. She might be Queen Victory's daughter by the airs she puts on; I 'd like to keep her myself if she was a little older, and I was n't goin' away from here."

"I s'pose they 'll make an awful row at being separated, won't they?" asked the younger woman.

"Oh, like as not; but they 'll have to have their row and get over it," said Mrs. Simmons easily. "You can take Timothy to the Orphan Asylum first, and then come back, and I 'll carry the baby to the Home of the Ladies' Relief and Protection Society; and if they yell they can yell, and take it out in yellin'; they won't get the best of Nancy Simmons."

"Don't talk so loud, Nancy, for mercy's sake. If the boy hears you, he 'll begin to take on, and we sha'n't get a wink of sleep. Don't let 'em know what you 're goin' to do with 'em till the last minute, or you 'll have trouble as sure as we sit here."

"Oh, they are sound asleep," responded Mrs. Simmons, with an uneasy look at the half-open door. "I went in and dragged a pillow out from under Timothy's head, and he never budged. He was sleepin' like a log, and so was Gay. Now, shut up, Et, and let me get three winks myself. You take the lounge, and I 'll stretch out in two chairs. Wake me up at eight o'clock, if I don't wake myself; for I 'm clean tired out with all this fussin' and plannin', and I feel stupid enough to sleep till kingdom come."

SCENE II.

Number Three, Minerva Court. First floor back.

LITTLE TIMOTHY JESSUP ASSUMES PARENTAL RESPONSIBILITIES.

WHEN the snores of the two watchers fell on the stillness of the death-chamber, with that cheerful regularity that betokens the sleep of the truly good, a little figure crept out of the bed in the adjoining room and closed the door noiselessly, but with trembling fingers; stealing then to the window to look out at the dirty street and the gray sky over which the first faint streaks of dawn were beginning to creep.

It was little Timothy Jessup (God alone knows whether he had any right to that special patronymic), but not the very same Tim Jessup who had kissed the baby Gay in her little crib, and gone to sleep on his own hard bed in that room, a few hours before. As he stood shivering at the window,

one thin hand hard pressed upon his heart
to still its beating, there was a light of sudden resolve in his eyes, a new-born look of
anxiety on his unchildlike face.

"I will not have Gay protectioned and
reliefed, and I will not be taken away from
her and sent to a 'sylum, where I can never
find her again!" and with these defiant
words trembling, half spoken, on his lips,
he glanced from the unconscious form in the
crib to the terrible door, which might open
at any moment and divide him from his
heart's delight, his darling, his treasure, his
only joy, his own, own baby Gay.

But what should he do? Run away: that
was the only solution of the matter, and no
very difficult one either. The cruel women
were asleep; the awful Thing that had
been Flossy would never speak again; and
no one else in Minerva Court cared enough
for them to pursue them very far or very
long.

"And so," thought Timothy swiftly, "I
will get things ready, take Gay, and steal
softly out of the back door, and run away
to the 'truly' country, where none of these
bad people ever can find us, and where I
can get a mother for Gay; somebody to

'dopt her and love her till I grow up a man and take her to live with me."

The moment this thought darted into Timothy's mind, it began to shape itself in definite action.

Gabrielle, or Lady Gay, as Flossy called her, in honor of her favorite stage heroine, had been tumbled into her crib half dressed the night before. The only vehicle kept for her use in the family stables was a clothes-basket, mounted on four wooden wheels and cushioned with a dingy shawl. A yard of clothes-line was tied on to one end, and in this humble conveyance the Princess would have to be transported from the Ogre's castle; for she was scarcely old enough to accompany the Prince on foot, even if he had dared to risk detection by waking her: so the clothes-basket must be her chariot, and Timothy her charioteer, as on many a less fateful expedition.

After he had changed his ragged nightgown for a shabby suit of clothes, he took Gay's one clean apron out of a rickety bureau drawer ("for I can never find a mother for her if she's too dirty," he thought), her Sunday hat from the same receptacle, and last of all a comb, and a

faded Japanese parasol that stood in a corner. These he deposited under the old
shawl that decorated the floor of the chariot.
He next groped his way in the dim light
toward a mantelshelf, and took down a sav-
ings - bank, — a florid little structure with
"Bank of England " stamped over the minia-
ture door, into which the jovial gentleman
who frequented the house often slipped
pieces of silver for the children, and into
which Flossy dipped only when she was in a
state of temporary financial embarrassment.
Timothy did not dare to jingle it; he could
only hope that as Flossy had not been in her
usual health of late (though in more than
her usual " spirits "), she had not felt
obliged to break the bank.

Now for provisions. There were plenty
of "funeral baked meats " in the kitchen;
and he hastily gathered a dozen cookies into
a towel, and stowed them in the coach with
the other sinews of war.

So far, well and good; but the worst was
to come. With his heart beating in his
bosom like a trip-hammer, and his eyes di-
lated with fear, he stepped to the door between the two rooms, and opened it softly.
Two thundering snores, pitched in such dif-

ferent keys that they must have proceeded
from two separate sets of nasal organs, reas-
sured the boy. He looked out into the alley.
" Not a creature was stirring, not even a
mouse." The Minerva Courtiers could n't
be owls and hawks too, and there was not
even the ghost of a sound to be heard. Satisfied that all was well, Timothy went back to
the bedroom, and lifted the battered clothes-
basket, trucks and all, in his slender arms,
carried it up the alley and down the street
a little distance, and deposited it on the
pavement beside a vacant lot. This done,
he sped back to the house. " How beauti-
fully they snore ! " he thought, as he stood
again on the threshold. " Shall I leave 'em
a letter ? . . . P'raps I better . . . and then
they won't follow us and bring us back." So
he scribbled a line on a bit of torn paper
bag, and pinned it on the enemies' door.

" A kind Lady is goin to Adopt
us it is a Grate ways off so do not
Hunt good by. Tim."

Now all was ready. No ; one thing more.
Timothy had been met in the street by a
pretty young girl a few weeks before. The

love of God was smiling in her heart, the love of children shining in her eyes; and she led him, a willing captive, into a mission Sunday-school near by. And so much in earnest was the sweet little teacher, and so hungry for any sort of good tidings was the starved little pupil, that Timothy "got religion" then and there, as simply and naturally as a child takes its mother's milk. He was probably in a state of crass ignorance regarding the Thirty-nine Articles; but it was the "engrafted word," of which the Bible speaks, that had blossomed in Timothy's heart; the living seed had always been there, waiting for some beneficent fostering influence; for he was what dear Charles Lamb would have called a natural "kingdom-of-heavenite." Thinking, therefore, of Miss Dora's injunction to pray over all the extraordinary affairs of life and as many of the ordinary ones as possible, he hung his tattered straw hat on the bedpost, and knelt beside Gay's crib with this whispered prayer : —

"*Our Father who art in heaven, please help me to find a mother for Gay, one that she can call Mamma, and another one for me, if there's enough, but not unless. Please excuse me for taking away the*

*clothes-basket, which does not exactly belong
to us ; but if I do not take it, dear heavenly
Father, how will I get Gay to the railroad?
And if I don't take the Japanese umbrella
she will get freckled, and nobody will adopt
her. No more at present, as I am in a
great hurry. Amen."*

He put on his hat, stooped over the sleeping baby, and took her in his faithful arms,
— arms that had never failed her yet. She
half opened her eyes, and seeing that she
was safe on her beloved Timothy's shoulder,
clasped her dimpled arms tight about his
neck, and with a long sigh drifted off again
into the land of dreams. Bending beneath
her weight, he stepped for the last time
across the threshold, not even daring to
close the door behind him.

Up the alley and round the corner he
sped, as fast as his trembling legs could
carry him. Just as he was within sight of
the goal of his ambition, that is, the chariot
aforesaid, he fancied he heard the sound of
hurrying feet behind him. To his fevered
imagination the tread was like that of an
avenging army on the track of the foe. He
did not dare to look behind. On! for the
clothes-basket and liberty! He would re-

linquish the Japanese umbrella, the cookies, the comb, and the apron, — all the booty, in fact, — as an inducement for the enemy to retreat, but he would never give up the prisoner.

On the feet hurried, faster and faster. He stooped to put Gay in the basket, and turned in despair to meet his pursuers, when a little, grimy, rough-coated, lop-eared, split-tailed thing, like an animated rag-bag, leaped upon his knees; whimpering with joy, and imploring, with every grace that his simple doggish heart could suggest, to be one of the eloping party.

Rags had followed them!

Timothy was so glad to find it no worse that he wasted a moment in embracing the dog, whose delirious joy at the prospect of this probably dinnerless and supperless expedition was ludicrously exaggerated. Then he took up the rope and trundled the chariot gently down a side street leading to the station.

Everything worked to a charm. They met only an occasional milk (and water) man, starting on his matutinal rounds, for it was now after four o'clock, and one or two cavaliers of uncertain gait, just return-

ing to their homes, several hours too late for
their own good ; but these gentlemen were
in no condition of mind to be over-inter-
ested, and the little fugitives were troubled
with no questions as to their intentions.

And so they went out into the world together, these three : Timothy Jessup (if it
was Jessup), brave little knight, nameless
nobleman, tracing his descent back to God,
the Father of us all, and bearing the Divine
likeness more than most of us; the little
Lady Gay, — somebody — nobody — anybody, — from nobody knows where, — des-
tination equally uncertain ; and Rags, of
pedigree most doubtful, scutcheon quite ob-
scured by blots, but a perfect gentleman,
true - hearted and loyal to the core, — in
fact, an angel in fur. These three, with the
clothes-basket as personal property and the
Bank of England as security, went out to
seek their fortune ; and, unlike Lot's wife,
without daring to look behind, shook the
dust of Minerva Court from off their feet
forever and forever.

SCENE III.

The Railway Station.

TIMOTHY PLANS A CAMPAIGN, AND PROVIDENCE ASSISTS MATERIALLY IN CARRYING IT OUT, OR VICE VERSA.

BY dint of skillful generalship, Timothy gathered his forces on a green bank just behind the railway depot, cleared away a sufficient number of tin cans and oyster-shells to make a flat space for the chariot of war, which had now become simply a cradle, and sat down, with Rags curled up at his feet, to plan the campaign.

He pushed back the ragged hat from his waving hair, and, clasping his knees with his hands, gazed thoughtfully at the towering chimneys in the foreground and the white-winged ships in the distant harbor. There was a glimpse of something like a man's purpose in the sober eyes; and as the morning sunlight fell upon his earnest face, the angel in him came to the surface, and

crowded the " boy part" quite out of sight,
as it has a way of doing sometimes with children.

How some father - heart would have
throbbed with pride to own him, and how
gladly lifted the too heavy burden from his
childish shoulders!

Timothy Jessup, aged ten or eleven, or
thereabouts (the records had not been kept
with absolute exactness) — Timothy Jessup,
somewhat ragged, all forlorn, and none too
clean at the present moment, was a poet,
philosopher, and lover of the beautiful. The
dwellers in Minerva Court had never discov-
ered the fact; for, although he had lived in
that world, he had most emphatically never
been of it. He was a boy of strange no-
tions, and the vocabulary in which he expressed them was stranger still; further-
more, he had gentle manners, which must
have been indigenous, as they had certainly
never been cultivated; and, although he had
been in the way of handling pitch for many
a day, it had been helpless to defile him,
such was the essential purity of his nature.

To find a home and a mother for Lady
Gay had been Timothy's secret longing ever
since he had heard people say that Flossy

might die. He had once enjoyed all the comforts of a Home with a capital H; but it was the cosy one with the little " h " that he so much desired for her.

Not that he had any ill treatment to remember in the excellent institution of which he was for several years an inmate. The matron was an amiable and hard-working woman, who wished to do her duty to all the children under her care ; but it would be an inspired human being indeed who could give a hundred and fifty motherless or fatherless children all the education and care and training they needed, to say nothing of the love that they missed and craved. What wonder, then, that an occasional hungry little soul, starved for want of something not provided by the management ; say, a morning cuddle in father's bed or a ride on father's knee, — in short, the sweet daily jumble of lap-trotting, gentle caressing, endearing words, twilight stories, motherly tucks-in-bed, good-night kisses, — all the dear, simple, every-day accompaniments of the home with the little " h."

Timothy Jessup, bred in such an atmosphere, would have gladdened every life that touched his at any point. Plenty of wistful

men and women would have thanked God
nightly on their knees for the gift of such a
son ; and here he was, sitting on a tin can,
bowed down with family cares, while thou·
sands of graceless little scalawags were slap-
ping the faces of their French nurse-maids
and bullying their parents, in that very city.
— Ah me !

As for the tiny Lady Gay, she had all the
winsome virtues to recommend her. No one
ever feared that she would die young out of
sheer goodness. You would not have loved
her so much for what she was as because
you could n't help yourself. This feat once
accomplished, she blossomed into a thousand
graces, each one more bewitching than the
last you noted.

Where, in the name of all the sacred laws
of heredity, did the child get her sunshiny
nature? Born in misery, and probably in
sin, nurtured in wretchedness and poverty, she had brought her "radiant morning visions" with her into the world. Like
Wordsworth's immortal babe, "with trail-
ing clouds of glory " had she come, from God
who was her home ; and the heaven that lies
about us all in our infancy, — that Garden
of Eden into which we are all born, like

the first man and the first woman, — that heaven lay about her still, stronger than the touch of earth.

What if the room were desolate and bare? The yellow sunbeams stole through the narrow window, and in the shaft of light they threw across the dirty floor Gay played, — oblivious of everything save the flickering golden rays that surrounded her.

The raindrops chasing each other down the dingy pane, the snowflakes melting softly on the casement, the brown leaf that the wind blew into her lap as she sat on the sidewalk, the chirp of the little beggar-sparrows over the cobblestones, all these brought as eager a light into her baby eyes as the costliest toy. With no earthly father or mother to care for her, she seemed to be God's very own baby, and He amused her in his own good way; first by locking her happiness within her own soul (the only place where it is ever safe for a single moment), and then by putting her under Timothy's paternal ministrations.

Timothy's mind traveled back over the past, as he sat among the tin cans and looked at Rags and Gay. It was a very small story, if he ever found any one who would

care to hear it. There was a long journey
in a great ship, a wearisome illness of many
weeks, — or was it months? — when his
curls had been cut off, and all his memories
with them; then there was the Home; then
there was Flossy, who came to take him
away; then — oh, bright, bright spot! oh,
blessed time! — there was baby Gay; then,
worse than all, there was Minerva Court.
But he did not give many minutes to remi-
niscence. He first broke open the Bank of
England, and threw it away, after finding to
his joy that their fortune amounted to one
dollar and eighty-five cents. This was so
much in advance of his expectations that he
laughed aloud; and Rags, wagging his tail
with such vigor that he nearly broke it in
two, jumped into the cradle and woke the
baby.

Then there was a happy family circle, you
may believe me, and with good reason, too!
A trip to the country (meals and lodging
uncertain, but that was a trifle), a sight of
green meadows, where Tim would hear real
birds sing in the trees, and Gay would
gather wild flowers, and Rags would chase,
and perhaps — who knows? — catch tooth-
some squirrels and fat little field-mice, of

which the country dogs visiting Minerva
Court had told the most mouth-watering
tales. Gay's transport knew no bounds.
Her child-heart felt no regret for the past,
no care for the present, no anxiety for the
future. The only world she cared for was
in her sight; and she had never, in her brief
experience, gazed upon it with more radiant
anticipation than on this sunny June morning, when she had opened her bright eyes on
a pleasant, odorous bank of oyster-shells, instead of on the accustomed surroundings of
Minerva Court.

Breakfast was first in order.

There was a pump conveniently near, and
the oyster-shells made capital cups. Gay
had three cookies, Timothy two, and Rags
one; but there was no statute of limitations
placed on the water; every one had as much
as he could drink.

The little matter of toilets came next.
Timothy took the dingy rag which did duty
for a handkerchief, and, calling the pump
again into requisition, scrubbed Gay's face
and hands tenderly, but firmly. Her clothes
were then all smoothed down tidily, but the
clean apron was kept for the eventful moment when her future mother should first

be allowed to behold the form of her adopted child.

The comb was then brought out, and her mop of red-gold hair was assisted to fall in wet spirals all over her lovely head, which always "wiggled" too much for any more formal style of hair-dressing. Her Sunday hat being tied on, as the crowning glory, this lucky little princess, this child of Fortune, so inestimably rich in her own opinion, this daughter of the gods, I say, was returned to the basket, where she endeavored to keep quiet until the next piece of delightful un-expectedness should rise from fairy-land upon her excited gaze.

Timothy and Rags now went to the pump, and Rags was held under the spout. This was a new and bitter experience, and he wished for a few brief moments that he had never joined the noble army of deserters, but had stayed where dirt was fashionable. Being released, the sense of abnormal clean-liness mounted to his brain, and he tore breathlessly round in a circle seventy-seven times without stopping. But this only dried his hair and amused Gay, who was begin-ning to find the basket confining, and who clamored for "Timfy" to take her to "yide."

Timothy attended to himself last, as usual.
He put his own head under the pump, and
scrubbed his face and hands heartily; wip-
ing them on his — well, he wiped them,
and that is the main thing; besides, his
handkerchief had been reduced to a pulp in
Gay's service. He combed his hair, pulled
up his stockings and tied his shoes neatly,
buttoned his jacket closely over his shirt,
and was just pinning up the rent in his hat,
when Rags considerately brought another
suggestion in the shape of an old chicken-
wing, with which he brushed every speck of
dust from his clothes. This done, and being
no respecter of persons, he took the family
comb to Rags, who woke the echoes during
the operation, and hoped to the Lord that
the squirrels would run slowly and that the
field-mice would be very tender, to pay him
for this.

It was now nearly eight o'clock, and the
party descended the hillside and entered the
side door of the station.

The day's work had long since begun, and
there was the usual din and uproar of railroad traffic. Trucks, laden high with boxes
and barrels, were being driven to the wide
doors, and porters were thundering and

thumping and lurching the freight from one
set of cars into another; their primary ob-
jects being to make a racket and demolish
raw material, thereby increasing manufac-
ture and export, but incidentally to load or
unload as much freight as possible in a given
time.

Timothy entered, trundling his carriage,
where Lady Gay sat enthroned like a Mur-
ray Hill belle on a dog-cart, conscious pride
of Sunday hat on week-day morning exud-
ing from every feature; and Rags followed
close behind, clean, but with a crushed spirit,
which he could stimulate only by the most
seductive imaginations. No one molested
them, for Timothy was very careful not to
get in any one's way. Finally, he drew up
in front of a high blackboard, on which the
names of various way-stations were printed
in gold letters : —

> CHESTERTOWN.
> SANDFORD.
> REEDVILLE.
> BINGHAM.
> SKAGGSTOWN.
> ESBURY.
> SCRATCH CORNER.
> HILLSIDE.

MOUNTAIN VIEW.

EDGEWOOD.

PLEASANT RIVER.

"The names get nicer and nicer as you read down the line, and the furtherest one of all is the very prettiest, so I guess we 'll go there," thought Timothy, not realizing that his choice was based on most insecure foundations; and that, for aught he knew, the milk of human kindness might have more cream on it at Scratch Corner than at Pleasant River, though the latter name was certainly more attractive.

Gay approved of Pleasant River, and so did Rags; and Timothy moved off down the station to a place on the open platform where a train of cars stood ready for starting, the engine at the head gasping and puffing and breathing as hard as if it had an acute attack of asthma.

"How much does it cost to go to Pleasant River, please?" asked Tim, bravely, of a kind-looking man in a blue coat and brass buttons, who stood by the cars.

"This is a freight train, sonny," replied the man; "takes four hours to get there. Better wait till 10.45; buy your ticket up in the station."

" 10.45 ! " Tim saw visions of Mrs. Simmons speeding down upon him in hot pursuit, kindled by Gay's disappearance into an appreciation of her charms.

The tears stood in his eyes as Gay clambered out of the basket, and danced with impatience, exclaiming, " Gay wants to yide now ! yide now ! yide now ! "

" Did you want to go sooner ? " asked the man, who seemed to be entirely too much interested in humanity to succeed in the railroad business. " Well, as you seem to have consid'rable of a family on your hands, I guess we 'll take you along. Jim, unlock that car and let these children in, and then lock it up again. It 's a car we 're taking up to the end of the road for repairs, bubby, so the comp'ny 'll give you and your folks a free ride ! "

Timothy thanked the man in his politest manner, and Gay pressed a piece of moist cooky in his hand, and offered him one of her swan's-down kisses, a favor of which she was usually as chary as if it had possessed a market value.

" Are you going to take the dog ? " asked the man, as Rags darted up the steps with sniffs and barks of ecstatic delight. " He ain't so handsome but you can get another easy enough!" (Rags held his breath in suspense, and wondered if he had been put under a roaring cataract, and then ploughed in deep furrows with a sharp-toothed instrument of torture, only to be left behind at last!)

"That's just why I take him," said Timothy; "because he is n't handsome and has nobody else to love him."

("Not a very polite reason," thought Rags; "but anything to go!")

"Well, jump in, dog and all, and they 'll give you the best free ride to the country you ever had in your life! Tell 'em it 's all right, Jim;" and the train steamed out of the depot, while the kind man waved his bandana handkerchief until the children were out of sight.

SCENE IV.

Pleasant River.

JABE SLOCUM ASSUMES THE RÔLE OF GUARDIAN ·ANGEL.

JABE SLOCUM had been down to Edge-wood, and was just returning to the White Farm, by way of the cross-roads and Hard Scrabble school-house. He was in no hurry, though he always had more work on hand than he could leave undone for a month; and Maria also was taking her own time, as usual, even stopping now and then to crop an unusually sweet tuft of grass that grew within smelling distance, and which no mare (with a driver like Jabe) could afford to pass without notice.

Jabe was ostensibly out on an " errant " for Miss Avilda Cummins; but, as he had been in her service for six years, she had no expectations of his accomplishing anything beyond getting to a place and getting back in the same day, the distance covered being no factor at all in the matter.

But one need n't go to Miss Avilda Cummins for a description of Jabe Slocum's peculiarities. They were all so written upon his face and figure and speech that the wayfaring man, though a fool, could not err in his judgment. He was a long, loose, knock-kneed, slack-twisted person, and would have been " longer yit if he hed n't hed so much turned up for feet," — so Aunt Hitty Tarbox said. (Aunt Hitty went from house to house in Edgewood and Pleasant River, making over boys' clothes ; and as her tongue flew as fast as her needle, her sharp speeches were always in circulation in both villages.)

Mr. Slocum had sandy hair, high cheekbones, a pair of kindly light blue eyes, and a most unique nose : I hardly know to what order of architecture it belonged, — perhaps Old Colonial would describe it as well as anything else. It was a wide, flat, well-ventilated, hospitable edifice (so to speak), so peculiarly constructed and applied that Samantha Ann Ripley (of whom more anon) declared that " the reason Jabe Slocum ketched cold so easy was that, if he did n't hold his head jess so, it kep' a-rainin' in ! "

His mouth was simply an enormous slit

in his face, and served all the purposes for
which a mouth is presumably intended, save,
perhaps, the trivial one of decoration. In
short (a ludicrously inappropriate word for
the subject), it was a capital medium for
exits and entrances, but no ornament to his
countenance. When Rhapsena Crabb, now
deceased, was first engaged to Jabez Slocum,
Aunt Hitty Tarbox said it beat her "how
Rhapseny ever got over Jabe's mouth;
though she could 'a' got intew it easy 'nough,
or raound it, if she took plenty o' time."
But perhaps Rhapsena appreciated a mouth
(in a husband) that never was given to
"jawin'," and which uttered only kind words
during her brief span of married life. And
there was precious little leisure for kissing
at Pleasant River!

As Jabe had passed the store, a few
minutes before, one of the boys had called
out, facetiously, "Shet yer mouth when ye
go by the deepot, Laigs; the train's comin'
in!" But he only smiled placidly, though
it was an ancient joke, the flavor of which
had just fully penetrated the rustic skull;
and the villagers could not resist titillating
the sense of humor with it once or twice a
month. Neither did Jabez mind being called

" Laigs," the local pronunciation of the word " legs ; " in fact, his good humor was too deep to be ruffled. His " cistern of wrathfulness was so small, and the supply pipe so unready," that it was next to impossible to " put him out," so the natives said.

He was a man of tolerable education ; the only son of his parents, who had endeavored to make great things of him, and might perhaps have succeeded, if he had n't always had so little time at his disposal, — had n't been " so drove," as he expressed it. He went to the village school as regularly as he could n't help, that is, as many days as he could n't contrive to stay away, until he was fourteen. From there he was sent to the Academy, three miles distant; but his mother soon found that he could n't make the two trips a day and be " under cover by candlelight ; " so the plan of a classical education was abandoned, and he was allowed to speed the home plough, — a profession which he pursued with such moderation that his father, when starting him down a furrow, used to hang his dinner-pail on his arm, and, bidding him good-by, beg him, with tears in his eyes, to be back before sundown.

At the present moment Jabe was enjoying a cud of Old Virginia plug tobacco, and
taking in no more of the landscape than he
could avoid, when Maria, having wound up
to the top of Marm Berry's hill, in spite of
herself walked directly out on one side of
the road, and stopped short to make room ·
for the passage of an imposing procession,
made up of one straw phaeton, one baby,
one strange boy, and one strange dog.

Jabe eyed the party with some placid interest, for he loved children, but with no
undue excitement. Shifting his huge quid,
he inquired in his usual leisurely manner,
" Which way yer goin', bub, — t' the Swamp
or t' the Falls ? "

Timothy thought neither sounded especially inviting, but, rapidly choosing the
lesser evil, replied, " To the Falls, sir."

" Thy way happens to be my way, 's
Rewth said to Naomi ; so 'f gittin' over the
road 's your objeck, 'n' y' ain't pertickler
'baout the gait ye travel, ye can git in 'n'
ride a piece. We don't b'lieve in hurryin',
Mariar 'n' me. Slow 'n' easy goes fur in a
day, 's our motto. Can ye git your folks
aboard withaout spillin' any of 'em ? "

No wonder he asked, for Gay was in such

a wild state of excitement that she could
hardly be held.

"I can lift Gay up, if you'll please take
her, sir," said Timothy; "and if you're
quite sure the horse will stand still."

"Bless your soul, she'll stan' all right;
she likes stan'in' a heap better 'n she doos
goin'; runnin' away ain't no temptation to
Maria Cummins; let well enough alone 's
her motto. Jump in, sissy! There ye be!
Now git yer baby-shay in the back of the
wagon, bubby, 'n' we'll be 's snug 's a bug
in a rug."

Timothy, whose creed was simple and
whose beliefs were crystal clear, now felt
that his morning prayer had been heard,
and that the Lord was on his side; so he
abandoned all idea of commanding the situation, and gave himself up to the full ecstasy
of the ride, as they jogged peacefully along
the river road.

Gay held a piece of a rein that peeped
from Jabe's colossal hand (which was said
by the villagers to cover most as much terri-
tory as the hand of Providence), and was
convinced that she was driving Maria, an
idea that made her speechless with joy.

Rags' wildest dreams of squirrels came

true; and, reconciled at length to cleanliness, he was capering in and out of the woods, thinking what an Arabian Nights' entertainment he would give the Minerva Court dogs when he returned, if return he ever must to that miserable, squirrelless hole.

The meadows on the other side of the river were gorgeous with yellow buttercups, and here and there a patch of blue iris or wild sage. The black cherry trees were masses of snowy bloom; the water at the river's edge held spikes of blue arrowweed in its crystal shallows; while the roadside itself was gay with daisies and feathery grasses.

In the midst of this loveliness flowed Pleasant River,   .

"Vexed in all its seaward course by bridges, dams, and mills,"

but finding time, during the busy summer months, to flush its fertile banks with beauty.

Suddenly (a word that could seldom be truthfully applied to the description of Jabe Slocum's movements) the reins were ruthlessly drawn from Lady Gay's hands and wound about the whipstock.

" Gorry ! " ejaculated Mr. Slocum, " ef
I hain't left the widder Foss settin' on Aunt
Hitty's hoss-block, 'n' I promised to pick her
up when I come along back ! That all comes
o' my drivin' by the store so fast on account
o' the boys hectorin' of me, so 't when I got
to the turn I was so kind of het up I jogged
right along the straight road. Haste makes
waste 's an awful good motto. Pile out,
young ones ! It's only half a mile from
here to the Falls, 'n' you 'll have to get there
on Shank's mare ! "

So saying, he dumped the astonished
children into the middle of the road, from
whence he had plucked them, turned the
docile mare, and with a " Git, Mariar ! "
went four miles back to relieve Aunt Hitty's
horse - block from the weight of the widder
Foss (which was no joke !).

This turn of affairs was most unexpected,
and Gay seemed on the point of tears ; but
Timothy gathered her a handful of wild
flowers, wiped the dust from her face, put
on the clean blue gingham apron, and established her in the basket, where she soon fell
asleep, wearied by the excitements of the
day.

Timothy's heart began to be a little trou⸴

bled as he walked on and on through the
leafy woods, trundling the basket behind
him. Nothing had gone wrong; indeed,
everything had been much easier than he
could have hoped. Perhaps it was the
weariness that had crept into his legs, and
the hollowness that began to appear in his
stomach; but, somehow, although in the
morning he had expected to find Gay's new
mothers beckoning from every window, so
that he could scarcely choose between them,
he now felt as if the whole race of mothers
had suddenly become extinct.

Soon the village came in sight, nestled in
the laps of the green hills on both sides of
the river. Timothy trudged bravely on,
scanning all the dwellings, but finding none
of them just the thing. At last he turned
deliberately off the main road, where the
houses seemed too near together and too
near the street, for his taste, and trundled
his family down a shady sort of avenue, over
which the arching elms met and clasped
hands.

Rags had by this time lowered his tail to
half-mast, and kept strictly to the beaten
path, notwithstanding manifold temptations
to forsake it. He passed two cats without

a single insulting remark, and his entire demeanor was eloquent of nostalgia.

"Oh, dear!" sighed Timothy disconsolately; "there's something wrong with all the places. Either there's no pigeon-house, like in all the pictures, or no flower garden, or no chickens, or no lady at the window, or else there's lots of baby-clothes hanging on the wash-lines. I don't believe I shall ever find " —

At this moment a large, comfortable white house, that had been heretofore hidden by great trees, came into view. Timothy drew nearer to the spotless picket fence, and gazed upon the beauties of the side yard and the front garden, — gazed and gazed, and fell desperately in love at first sight.

The whole thing had been made as if to order; that is all there is to say about it. There was an orchard, and, oh, ecstasy! what hosts of green apples! There was an interesting grindstone under one tree, and a bright blue chair and stool under another; a thicket of currant and gooseberry bushes; and a flock of young turkeys ambling awkwardly through the barn. Timothy stepped gently along in the thick grass, past a pump and a mossy trough, till a side porch came

into view, with a woman sitting there sewing
bright-colored rags. A row of shining tin
pans caught the sun's rays, and threw them
back in a thousand glittering prisms of light;
the grasshoppers and crickets chirped sleepily
in the warm grass, and a score of tiny yellow
butterflies hovered over a group of odorous
hollyhocks.

Suddenly the person on the porch broke
into this cheerful song, which she pitched in
so high a key and gave with such emphasis
that the crickets and grasshoppers retired
by mutual consent from any further compe-
tition, and the butterflies suspended opera-
tions for several seconds : —

> " I 'll chase the antelope over the plain,
> The tiger's cub I 'll bind with a chain,
> And the wild gazelle with the silv'ry feet
> I 'll bring to thee for a playmate sweet."

Timothy listened intently for some moments, but could not understand the words,
unless the lady happened to be in the
menagerie business, which he thought un-
likely, but delightful should it prove true.

His eye then fell on a little marble slab
under a tree in a shady corner of the orchard.

"That 's a country doorplate," he thought;

" yes, it 's got the lady's name, ' Martha Cummins,' printed on it. Now I 'll know what to call her."

He crept softly on to the front side of the house. There were flower beds, a lovable white cat snoozing on the doorsteps, and — a lady sitting at the open window knitting !

At this vision Timothy's heart beat so hard against his little jacket that he could only stagger back to the basket, where Rags and Lady Gay were snuggled together, fast asleep. He anxiously scanned Gay's face; moistened his rag of a handkerchief at the only available source of supply; scrubbed an atrocious dirt spot from the tip of her spirited nose; and then, dragging the basket along the path leading to the front gate, he opened it and went in, mounted the steps, plied the brass knocker, and waited in child-like faith for a summons to enter and make himself at home.

SCENE V.

The White Farm.   Afternoon.

TIMOTHY FINDS A HOUSE IN WHICH HE THINKS
A BABY IS NEEDED, BUT THE INMATES DO NOT
ENTIRELY AGREE WITH HIM.

MEANWHILE, Miss Avilda Cummins had
left her window and gone into the next room
for a skein of yarn. She answered the
knock, however; and, opening the door,
stood rooted to the threshold in speechless
astonishment, very much as if she had seen
the shades of her ancestors drawn up in line
in the dooryard.

Off went Timothy's hat. He had n't seen
the lady's face very clearly when she was
knitting at the window, or he would never
have dared to knock; but it was too late to
retreat. Looking straight into her cold eyes
with his own shining gray ones, he said
bravely, but with a trembling voice, " Do
you need any babies here, if you please ? "
(Need any babies! What an inappropriate,

nonsensical expression, to be sure ; as if a baby were something exquisitely indispensable, like the breath of life, for instance !)

No answer. Miss Vilda was trying to assume command of her scattered faculties and find some clue to the situation. Timothy concluded that she was not, after all, the lady of the house ; and, remembering the marble doorplate in the orchard, tried again. " Does Miss Martha Cummins live here, if you please ? " (Oh, Timothy ! what induced you, in this crucial moment of your life, to touch upon that sorest spot in Miss Vilda's memory ?)

" What do you want ? " she faltered.

" I want to get somebody to adopt my baby," he said ; " if you have n't got any of your own, you could n't find one half as dear and as pretty as she is ; and you need n't have me too, you know, unless you should need me to help take care of her."

" You 're very kind," Miss Avilda answered sarcastically, preparing to shut the door upon the strange child ; " but I don't think I care to adopt any babies this afternoon, thank you. You 'd better run right back home to your mother, if you 've got one, and know where 't is, anyhow."

" I — have n't ! " cried poor Timothy, with a sudden and unpremeditated burst of tears at the failure of his hopes ; for he was half child as well as half hero. At this juncture Gay opened her eyes, and burst into a wild howl at the unwonted sight of Timothy's grief ; and Rags, who was full of exquisite sensibility, and quite ready to weep with those who did weep, lifted up his woolly head and added his piteous wails to the concert. It was a *tableau vivant.*

" Samanthy Ann ! " called Miss Vilda excitedly ; " Samanthy Ann ! Come right here and tell me what to do ! "

The person thus adjured flew in from the porch, leaving a serpentine trail of red, yellow, and blue rags in her wake. " Land o' liberty ! " she exclaimed, as she surveyed the group. " Where 'd they come from, and what air they tryin' to act out ? "

" This boy 's a baby agent, as near as I can make out ; he wants I should adopt this red-headed baby, but says I ain't obliged to take him too, and makes out they have n't got any home. I told him I wa'n't adoptin' any babies just now, and at that he burst out cryin', and the other two followed suit. Now, have the three of 'em just escaped from some asylum, or are they too little to be lunatics?"

Timothy dried his tears, in order that Gay should be comforted and appear at her best, and said penitently: "I cried before I thought, because Gay has n't had anything but cookies since last night, and she 'll have no place to sleep unless you 'll let us stay here just till morning. We went by all the other houses, and chose this one because everything was so beautiful."

"Nothin' but cookies sence — Land o' liberty!" ejaculated Samantha Ann, starting for the kitchen.

"Come back here, Samanthy! Don't you leave me alone with 'em, and don't let 's have all the neighbors runnin' in ; you take 'em into the kitchen and give 'em somethin' to eat, and we 'll see about the rest afterwards."

Gay kindled at the first casual mention of food ; and, trying to clamber out of the basket, fell over the edge, thumping her head smartly on the stone steps. Miss Vilda covered her face with her hands, and waited shudderingly for another yell, as the child's carnation stocking and terra-cotta head mingled wildly in the air. But Lady Gay disentangled herself, and laughed the merriest burst of laughter that ever woke the echoes. That was a joke; her life was full of them, served fresh every day; for no sort of adversity could long have power over such a nature as hers. "Come get supper," she cooed, putting her hand in Samantha's; adding that the "nasty lady need n't come," a remark that happily escaped detection, as it was rendered in very unintelligible "early English."

Miss Avilda tottered into the darkened sitting-room and sank on to a black hair-cloth sofa, while Samantha ushered the wanderers into the sunny kitchen, muttering to herself: "Wall, I vow! travelin' over the country all alone, 'n' not knee-high to a toad! They're sendin' out awful young tramps this season, but they sha'n't go away hungry, if I know it."

Accordingly, she set out a plentiful supply of bread and butter, gingerbread, pie, and milk, put a tin plate of cold hash in the shed for Rags, and swept him out to it with a corn broom; and, telling the children comfortably to cram their "everlastin' little bread-baskets full," returned to the sitting-room.

"Now, whatever makes you so panicky, Vildy? Did n't you never see a tramp before, for pity's sake? And if you 're scar't for fear I can't handle 'em alone, why, Jabe 'll be comin' along soon. The prospeck of gittin' to bed 's the only thing that 'll make him 'n' Maria hurry; 'n' they 'll both be cal'latin' on that by this time!"

"Samanthy Ann, the first question that that boy asked me was, 'If Miss Martha Cummins lived here.' Now, what do you make of that?"

Samantha looked as astonished as anybody could wish. "Asked if Marthy Cummins lived here? How under the canopy did he ever hear Marthy's name? Wall, somebody told him to ask, that 's all there is about it; and what harm was there in it, anyhow?"

"Oh, I don't know, I don't know; but the minute that boy looked up at me and asked for Martha Cummins, the old trouble, that I thought was dead and buried years ago, started right up in my heart and begun to ache just as if it all happened yesterday."

"Now keep stiddy, Vildy; what could happen?" urged Samantha.

"Why, it flashed across my mind in a

minute," and here Miss Vilda lowered her voice to a whisper, " that perhaps Martha's baby did n't die, as they told her."

" But, land o' liberty, s'posin' it did n't! Poor Marthy died herself more 'n twenty years ago."

" I know; but supposing her baby did n't die; and supposing it grew up and died, and left this little girl to roam round the world afoot and alone?"

" You 're cal'latin' dreadful close, 'pears to me; now, don't go s'posin' any more things. You 're makin' out one of them yellow-covered books, sech as the summer boarders bring out here to read; always chock full of doin's that never would come to pass in this or any other Christian country. You jest lay down and snuff your camphire, an' I 'll go out an' pump that boy drier 'n a sand heap!"

Now, Miss Avilda Cummins was unmarried by every implication of her being, as Henry James would say: but Samantha Ann Ripley was a spinster purely by accident. She had seldom been exposed to the witcheries of children, or she would have known long before this that, so far as she was personally concerned, they would always prove irresistible. She marched into the kitchen like a general resolved upon the extinction of the enemy. She walked out again, half an hour later, with the very teeth of her resolve drawn, but so painlessly that she had not been aware of the operation! She marched in a woman of a single purpose; she came out a double-faced diplomatist, with the seeds of sedition and conspiracy lurking, all unsuspected, in her heart.

The cause? Nothing more than a dozen trifles as " light as air." Timothy had sat upon a little wooden stool at her feet; and, resting his arms on her knees, had looked up into her kind, rosy face with a pair of liquid eyes like gray-blue lakes, eyes which seemed and were the very windows of his soul. He had sat there telling his wee bit of a story; just a vague, shadowy, plaintive, uncomplaining scrap of a story, without beginning, plot, or ending, but every word in it set Samantha Ann Ripley's heart throbbing.

And Gay, who knew a good thing when she saw it, had climbed up into her capacious lap, and, not being denied, had cuddled her head into that " gracious hollow " in Sa-

mantha's shoulder, that had somehow missed
the pressure of the childish heads that should
have lain there. Then Samantha's arm had
finally crept round the wheedlesome bit of
soft humanity, and before she knew it her
chair was swaying gently to and fro, to and
fro, to and fro; and the wooden rockers
creaked more sweetly than ever they had
creaked before, for they were singing their
first cradle song!

Then Gay heaved a great sigh of unspeakable satisfaction, and closed her lovely eyes.
She had been born with a desire to be cuddled, and had had precious little experience
of it. At the sound of this happy sigh and
the sight of the child's flower face, with the
upward curling lashes on the pink cheeks
and the moist tendrils of hair on the white
forehead, and the helpless, clinging touch of
the baby arm about her neck, I cannot tell
you the why or wherefore, but old memories and new desires began to stir in Samantha Ann Ripley's heart. In short, she
had met the enemy, and she was theirs!

Presently Gay was laid upon the old-
fashioned settle, and Samantha stationed
herself where she could keep the flies off her
by waving a palm-leaf fan.

" Now, there's one thing more I want you to tell me," said she, after she had possessed herself of Timothy's unhappy past, uncertain present, and still more dubious future; "and that is, what made you ask for Miss Marthy Cummins when you come to the door?"

" Why, I thought it was the lady-of-the-house's name," said Timothy; " I saw it on her doorplate."

" But we ain't got any doorplate, to begin with."

" Not a silver one on your door, like they have in the city; but isn't that white marble piece in the yard a doorplate? It's got ' Martha Cummins, aged 17,' on it. I thought may be in the country they had them in their gardens; only I thought it was queer they put their ages on them, because they'd have to be scratched out every little while, wouldn't they?"

" My grief!" ejaculated Samantha; "for pity's sake, don't you know a tombstun when you see it?"

" No; what is a tombstun?"

" Land sakes! what do you know, any way? Didn't you never see a graveyard where folks is buried?"

" I never went to the graveyard, but I

know where it is, and I know about people's
being buried. Flossy is going to be buried.
And so the white stone shows the places
where the people are put, and tells their
names, does it? Why, it is a kind of a
doorplate, after all, don't you see? Who is
Martha Cummins, aged 17?"

"She was Miss Vildy's sister, and she
went to the city, and then come home and
died here, long years ago. Miss Vildy set
great store by her, and can't bear to have
her name spoke; so remember what I say.
Now, this 'Flossy' you tell me about (of
all the fool names I ever hearn tell of, that
beats all, — sounds like a wax doll, with
her clo'se sewed on!), was she a young woman?"

"I don't know whether she was young or
not," said Tim, in a puzzled tone. "She
had young yellow hair, and very young
shiny teeth, white as china; but her neck
was crackled underneath, like Miss Vilda's;
— it had no kissing places in it like
Gay's."

"Well, you stay here in the kitchen a
spell now, 'n' don't let in that rag-dog o'
yourn till he stops scratchin', if he keeps it
up till the crack o' doom; — he's got to be

learned better manners.   Now, I'll go in 'n'
talk to Miss Vildy.   She may keep you over
night, 'n' she may not; I ain't noways sure.
You started in wrong foot foremost."

SCENE VI.

The White Farm.   Evening.

TIMOTHY, LADY GAY, AND RAGS PROVE FAITH-
FUL TO EACH OTHER.

SAMANTHA went into the sitting - room
and told the whole story to Miss Avilda;
told it simply and plainly, for she was not
given to arabesques in language, and then
waited for a response.

"Well, what do you advise doin'?"
asked Miss Cummins nervously.

"I don't feel comp'tent to advise, Vilda;
the house ain't mine, nor yet the beds
that's in it, nor the victuals in the butt'ry;
but as a professin' Christian and member of
the Orthodox Church in good and reg'lar
standin' you can't turn 'em ou'doors when
it's comin' on dark and they ain't got no
place to sleep."

"Plenty of good Orthodox folks turned
their backs on Martha when she was in trouble."

"There may be Orthodox hogs, for all I know," replied the blunt Samantha, who frequently called spades shovels in her search after absolute truth of statement, "but that ain't no reason why we should copy after 'em 's I know of."

"I don't propose to take in two strange children and saddle myself with 'em for days, or weeks, perhaps," said Miss Cummins coldly, "but I tell you what I will do. Supposing we send the boy over to Squire Bean's. It's near hayin' time, and he may take him in to help round and do chores. Then we'll tell him before he goes that we'll keep the baby as long as he gets a chance to work anywheres near. That will give us a chance to look round for some place for 'em and find out whether they've told us the truth."

"And if Squire Bean won't take him?" asked Samantha, with as much cold indifference as she could assume.

"Well, I suppose there's nothing for it but he must come back here and sleep. I'll go out and tell him so, — I declare I feel as weak as if I'd had a spell of sickness!"

Timothy bore the news better than Samantha had feared. Squire Bean's farm

did not look so very far away; his heart
was at rest about Gay and he felt that he
could find a shelter for himself somewhere.

"Now, how'll the baby act when she
wakes up and finds you're gone?" inquired
Miss Vilda anxiously, as Timothy took his
hat and bent down to kiss the sleeping child.

"Well, I don't know exactly," answered
Timothy, "because she's always had me,
you see. But I guess she'll be all right, now
that she knows you a little, and if I can see
her every day. She never cries except once
in a long while when she gets mad; and if
you're careful how you behave, she'll hardly
ever get mad at you."

"Well I vow!" exclaimed Miss Vilda
with a grim glance at Samantha, "I guess
she'd better do the behavin'."

So Timothy was shown the way across
the fields to Squire Bean's. Samantha ac-
companied him to the back gate, where she
gave him three doughnuts and a sneaking
kiss, watching him out of sight under the
pretense of taking the towels and napkins
off the grass.

It was nearly nine o'clock and quite dark
when Timothy stole again to the little gate

of the White Farm. The feet that had traveled so courageously over the mile walk to Squire Bean's had come back again slowly and wearily; for it is one thing to be shod with the sandals of hope, and quite another to tread upon the leaden soles of disappointment.

He leaned upon the white picket gate listening to the chirp of the frogs and looking at the fireflies as they hung their gleaming lamps here and there in the tall grass. Then he crept round to the side door, to implore the kind offices of the mediator before he entered the presence of the judge whom he assumed to be sitting in awful state somewhere in the front part of the house. He lifted the latch noiselessly and entered. Oh horror! Miss Avilda herself was sprinkling clothes at the great table on one side of the room. There was a moment of silence.

"He would n't have me," said Timothy simply, "he said I was n't big enough yet. I offered him Gay, too, but he did n't want her either, and if you please, I would rather sleep on the sofa so as not to be any more trouble."

"You won't do any such thing," responded Miss Vilda briskly. "You 've got a royal welcome this time sure, and I guess you can earn your lodging fast enough. You hear that?" and she opened the door that led into the upper part of the house.

A piercing shriek floated down into the kitchen, and another on the heels of that, and then another. Every drop of blood in Timothy's spare body rushed to his pale grave face. "Is she being whipped?" he whispered, with set lips.

"No; she needs it bad enough, but we ain't savages. She's only got the pretty temper that matches her hair, just as you said. I guess we have n't been behavin' to suit her."

"Can I go up? She'll stop in a minute when she sees me. She never went to bed without me before, and truly, truly, she's not a cross baby!"

"Come right along and welcome; just so long as she has to stay you 're invited to visit with her. Land sakes! the neighbors will think we 're killin' pigs!" and Miss Vilda started upstairs to show Timothy the way.

Gay was sitting up in bed and the faithful Samantha Ann was seated beside her with a lapful of useless bribes, — apples, seed-cakes, an illustrated Bible, a thermometer, an ear of red corn, and a large stuffed green bird, the glory of the "keeping room" mantelpiece.

But a whole aviary of highly colored songsters would not have assuaged Gay's woe at that moment. Every effort at conciliation was met with the one plaint: "I want my Timfy! I want my Timfy!"

At the first sight of the beloved form, Gay flung the sacred bird into the furthest corner of the room and burst into a wild sob of delight, as she threw herself into Timothy's loving arms.

Fifteen minutes later peace had descended on the troubled homestead, and Samantha went into the sitting-room and threw herself into the depths of the high-backed rocker. "Land o' liberty! perhaps I ain't het-up!" she ejaculated, as she wiped the sweat of honest toil from her brow and fanned herself vigorously with her apron. "I tell you what, at five o'clock I was dreadful sorry I had n't took Dave Milliken, but now I'm plaguey glad I did n't! Still" (and here she tried to smooth the green bird's ruffled plumage and restore him to his perch under the revered glass case), "still, children will be children."

"Some of 'em's considerable more like wild cats," said Miss Avilda briefly.

"You just go upstairs now, and see if you find anything that looks like wild cats; but 't any rate, wild cats or tame cats, we would n't dass turn 'em ou'doors this time o' night for fear of flyin' in the face of Providence. If it's a stint He's set us, I don't see but we've got to work it out somehow."

"I 'd rather have some other stint."

"To be sure!" retorted Samantha vigorously. "I never see anybody yet that did n't want to pick out her own stint; but mebbe if we got just the one we wanted it would n't be no stint! Land o' liberty, what 's that!"

There was a crash of falling tin pans, and Samantha flew to investigate the cause. About ten minutes later she returned, more heated than ever, and threw herself for the second time into the high-backed rocker.

"That dog's been givin' me a chase, I can tell you! He clawed and scratched so in the shed that I put him in the wood-house; and he went and clim' up on that carpen-

ter's bench, and pitched out that little winder at the top, and fell on to the milk-pan
shelf and scattered every last one of 'em,
and then upsot all my cans of termatter
plants. But I could n't find him, high nor
low. All to once I see by the dirt on the
floor that he 'd squirmed himself through
the skeeter-nettin' door int' the house, and
then I surmised where he was. Sure enough,
I crep' upstairs and there he was, layin'
between the two children as snug as you
please. He was snorin' like a pirate when
I found him, but when I stood over the bed
with a candle I could see 't his wicked little
eyes was wide open, and he was jest makin'
b'lieve sleep in hopes I 'd leave him where
he was. Well, I yanked him out quicker
'n scat, 'n' locked him in the old chicken
house, so I guess he 'll stay out, now. For
folks that claim to be no blood relation, I
declare him 'n' the boy 'n' the baby beats
anything I ever come across for bein' fond
of one 'nother!"

There were dreams at the White Farm
that night. Timothy went to sleep with a
prayer on his lips; a prayer that God would
excuse him for speaking of Martha's doorplate, and a most imploring postscript to the

effect that God would please make Miss
Vilda into a mother for Gay; thinking as
he floated off into the land of Nod, "It'll
be awful hard work, but I don't suppose He
cares how hard 't is!"

Lady Gay dreamed of driving beautiful
white horses beside sparkling waters . . .
and through flowery meadows. . . . And
great green birds perched on all the trees
and flew towards her as if to peck the cher-
ries of her lips . . . but when she tried to
beat them off they all turned into Timothys
and she hugged them close to her heart. . . .

Rags' visions were gloomy, for he knew
not whether the Lady with the Firm Hand
would free him from his prison in the morning, or whether he was there for all time.
. . . But there were intervals of bliss when
his fancies took a brighter turn . . . when
Hope smiled . . . and he bit the white cat's
tail . . . and chased the infant turkeys . . .
and found sweet, juicy, delicious bones in
unexpected places . . . and even inhaled,
in exquisite anticipation, the fragrance of
one particularly succulent bone that he had
hidden under Miss Vilda's bed.

Sleep carried Samantha so many years
back into the past that she heard the blithe

din of carpenters hammering and sawing on
a little house that was to be hers, his, *theirs.*
. . . And as she watched them, with all
sorts of maidenly hopes about the home
that was to be . . . some one stole up behind and caught her at it, and she ran away
blushing . . . and some one followed her
. . . and they watched the carpenters together. . . . Somebody else lived in the little house now, and Samantha never blushed
any more, but that part was mercifully hidden in the dream.

Miss Vilda's slumber was troubled. She
seemed to be walking through peaceful
meadows, brown with autumn, when all at
once there rose in the path steep hills and
rocky mountains. . . . She felt too tired and
too old to climb, but there was nothing else
to be done. . . . And just as she began the
toilsome ascent, a little child appeared, and
catching her helplessly by the skirts im-
plored to be taken with her. . . . And she
refused and went on alone . . . but, miracle
of miracles, when she reached the crest of
the first hill the child was there before her,
still beseeching to be carried. . . . And
again she refused, and again she wearily
climbed the heights alone, always meeting

the child when she reached their summits,
and always enacting the same scene. . . .
At last she cried in despair, "Ask me no
more, for I have not even strength enough
for my own needs!" . . . And the child
said, "I will help you;" and straightway
crept into her arms and nestled there as one
who would not be denied . . . and she took
up her burden and walked. . . . And as she
climbed the weight grew lighter and lighter,
till at length the clinging arms seemed to
give her peace and strength . . . and when
she neared the crest of the highest mountain
she felt new life throbbing in her veins and
new hopes stirring in her heart, and she remembered no more the pain and weariness
of her journey. . . . And all at once a
bright angel appeared to her and traced the
letters of a word upon her forehead and took
the child from her arms and disappeared.
. . . And the angel had the lovely smile
and sad eyes of Martha . . . and the word
she traced on Miss Vilda's forehead was
"Inasmuch"!

SCENE VII.

The Old Homestead.

MISTRESS AND MAID FIND TO THEIR AMAZE-
MENT THAT A CHILD, MORE THAN ALL OTHER
GIFTS, BRINGS HOPE WITH IT AND FORWARD
LOOKING THOUGHTS.

IT was called the White Farm, not because that was an unusual color in Pleasant
River. Nineteen out of every twenty houses
in the village were painted white, for it
had not then entered the casual mind that
any other course was desirable or possible.
Occasionally, a man of riotous imagination
would substitute two shades of buff, or make
the back of his barn red, but the spirit of
invention stopped there, and the majority of
sane people went on painting white. But
Miss Avilda Cummins was blessed with a
larger income than most of the inhabitants
of Pleasant River, and all her buildings,
the great house, the sheds, the carriage and
dairy houses, the fences and the barn, were
always kept in a state of dazzling purity;

"as if," the neighbors declared, "S'manthy Ann Ripley went over 'em every morning with a dust-cloth."

It was merely an accident that the carriage and work horses chanced to be white, and that the original white cats of the family kept on having white kittens to decorate the front doorsteps. It was not accident, however, but design, that caused Jabe Slocum to scour the country for a good white cow and persuade Miss Cummins to swap off the old red one, so that the "critters" in the barn should match.

Miss Avilda had been born at the White Farm; father and mother had been taken from there to the old country churchyard, and "Martha, aged 17," poor, pretty, willful Martha, the greatest pride and greatest sorrow of the family, was lying under the apple trees in the garden.

Here also the little Samantha Ann Ripley had come as a child years ago, to be playmate, nurse, and companion to Martha, and here she had stayed ever since, as friend, adviser, and "company-keeper" to the lonely Miss Cummins. Nobody in Pleasant River would have dared to think of her as anybody's "hired help," though she did receive

bed and board, and a certain sum yearly for
her services; but she lived with Miss Cummins on equal terms, as was the custom in
the good old New England villages, doing
the lion's share of the work, and marking
her sense of the situation by washing the
dishes while Miss Avilda wiped them, and
by never suffering her to feed the pig or go
down cellar.

Theirs had been a dull sort of life, in
which little had happéned to make them
grow into sympathy with the outside world.
All the sweetness of Miss Avilda's nature
had turned to bitterness and gall after
Martha's disgrace, sad home-coming, and
death. There had been much to forgive,
and she had not had the grace nor the
strength to forgive it until it was too late.
The mystery of death had unsealed her eyes,
and there had been a moment when the sad
and bitter woman might have been drawn
closer to the great Father - heart, there to
feel the throb of a Divine compassion that
would have sweetened the trial and made
the burden lighter. But the minister of the
parish proved a sorry comforter and adviser
in these hours of trial. The Reverend
Joshua Beckwith, whose view of God's uni-

verse was about as broad as if he had lived
on the inside of his own pork-barrel, had
cherished certain strong and unrelenting
opinions concerning Martha's final destina-
tion, which were not shared by Miss Cummins. Martha, therefore, was not laid with
the elect, but was put to rest in the orchard,
under the kindly, untheological shade of the
apple trees ; and they scattered their tinted
blossoms over her little white headstone, shed
their fragrance about her quiet grave, and
dropped their ruddy fruit in the high grass
that covered it, just as tenderly and respect-
fully as if they had been regulation willows.
The Reverend Joshua thus succeeded in drying up the springs of human sympathy in
Miss Avilda's heart when most she needed
comfort and gentle teaching ; and, distrust-
ing God for the moment, as well as his in-
exorable priest, she left her place in the old
meeting-house where she had " worshiped "
ever since she had acquired adhesiveness
enough to stick to a pew, and was not seen
there again for many years. The Reverend
Joshua had died, as all men must and as
most men should ; and a mild-voiced succes-
sor reigned in his place ; so the Cummins
pew was occupied once more.

Samantha Ann Ripley had had her heart history too, — one of a different kind. She had " kept company " with David Milliken for a little matter of twenty years, off and on, and Miss Avilda had expected at various times to lose her friend and helpmate ; but fear of this calamity had at length been quite put to rest by the fourth and final rupture of the bond, five years before.

There had always been a family feud between the Ripleys and the Millikens ; and when the young people took it into their heads to fall in love with each other in spite of precedent or prejudice, they found that the course of true love ran in anything but a smooth channel. It was, in fact, a sort of village Montague and Capulet affair ; but David and Samantha were no Romeo and Juliet. The climate and general conditions of life at Pleasant River were not favorable to the development of such exotics. The old people interposed barriers between the young ones as long as they lived ; and when they died, Dave Milliken's spirit was broken, and he began to annoy the valiant Samantha by what she called his " meechin' " ways. In one of his moments of weakness he took a widowed sister to live with him, a certain

Mrs. Pettigrove, of Edgewood, who inherited the Milliken objection to Ripleys, and who widened the breach and brought Samantha to the point of final and decisive rupture. The last straw was the statement, sown broadcast by Mrs. Pettigrove, that " Samanthy Ann Ripley's father never would 'a' died if he 'd ever had any doctorin' ; but 't was the gospel truth that they never had nobody to 'tend him but a hom'pathy man from Scratch Corner, who, of course, bein' a hom'path, did n't know no more about doctorin' 'n Cooper's cow."

Samantha told David after this that she did n't want to hear him open his mouth again, nor none of his folks ; that she was through with the whole lot of 'em forever and ever, 'n' she wished to the Lord she 'd had sense enough to put her foot down fifteen years ago, 'n' she hoped he 'd enjoy bein' tread underfoot for the rest of his natural life, 'n' she would n't speak to him again if she met him in her porridge dish." She then slammed the door and went upstairs to cry as if she were sixteen, as she watched him out of sight. Poor Dave Milliken ! just sweet and earnest and strong enough to suffer at being worsted by circumstances,

but never quite strong enough to conquer
them.

And it was to this household that Timothy had brought his child for adoption.

When Miss Avilda opened her eyes, the
morning after the arrival of the children,
she tried to remember whether anything
had happened to give her such a strange
feeling of altered conditions. It was Saturday, — baking day, — that could n't be it;
and she gazed at the little dimity-curtained
window and at the picture of the Death-bed
of Calvin, and wondered what was the matter.

Just then a child's laugh, bright, merry,
tuneful, infectious, rang out from some distant room, and it all came back to her as
Samantha Ann opened the door and peered
in.

"I 've got breakfast 'bout ready," she
said; " but I wish, soon 's you 're dressed,
you 'd step down 'n' see to it, 'n' let me
wash the baby. I guess water was skerse
where she come from!"

" They 're awake, are they?"

"Awake? Land o' liberty! As soon as
't was light, and before the boy had opened

his eyes, Gay was up 'n' poundin' on all the doors, 'n' hollorin' 'S'manfy' (beats all how she got holt o' my name so quick!), so 't I thought sure she'd disturb your sleep. See here, Vildy, we want those children should look respectable the few days they're here. I don't see how we can rig out the boy, but there's those old things of Marthy's in the attic; seems like it might be a blessin' on 'em if we used 'em this way."

"I thought of it myself in the night," answered Vilda briefly. "You'll find the key of the trunk in the light stand drawer. You see to the children, and I'll get breakfast on the table. Has Jabe come?"

"No; he sent a boy to milk, 'n' said he'd be right along. You know what that means!"

Miss Vilda moved about the immaculate kitchen, frying potatoes and making tea, setting on extra portions of bread and doughnuts and a huge pitcher of milk; while various noises, strange enough in that quiet house, floated down from above.

"This is dreadful hard on Samanthy," she reflected. "I don't know's I'd ought to have put it on her, knowing how she hates confusion and company, and all that;

but she seemed to think we'd got to tough it out for a spell, any way; though I don't expect her temper'll stand the strain very long."

The fact was, Samantha was banging doors and slatting tin pails about furiously to keep up an ostentatious show of ill humor. She tried her best to grunt with displeasure when Gay, seated in a wash-tub, crowed and beat the water with her dimpled hands, so that it splashed all over the carpet; but all the time there was such a joy tugging at her heart-strings as they had not felt for years.

When the bath was over, clean petticoats and ankle-ties were chosen out of the old leather trunk, and finally a little blue and white lawn dress. It was too long in the skirt, and pending the moment when Samantha should " take a tack in it," it antici· pated the present fashion, and made Lady Gay look more like a disguised princess than ever. The gown was low-necked and short-sleeved, in the old style; and Samantha was in despair till she found some little em-broidered muslin capes and full undersleeves, with which she covered Gay's pink neck and arms. These things of beauty so wrought upon the child's excitable nature that she could hardly keep still long enough to have her hair curled; and Samantha, as the shining rings dropped off her horny forefinger, was wrestling with the Evil One, in the shape of a little box of jewelry that she had found with the clothing. She knew that the wish was a vicious one, and that such gewgaws were out of place on a little pauper just taken in for the night; but her fingers trembled with a desire to fasten the little gold ears of corn on the shoulders, or tie the strings of coral beads round the child's pretty throat.

When the toilet was completed, and Samantha was emptying the tub, Gay climbed on the bureau and imprinted sloppy kisses of sincere admiration on the radiant reflection of herself in the little looking-glass; then, getting down again, she seized her heap of Minerva Court clothes, and, before the astonished Samantha could interpose, flung them out of the second-story window, where they fell on the top of the lilac bushes.

" Me does n't like nasty old dress," she explained, with a dazzling smile that was a justification in itself; " me likes pretty new dress!" and then, with one hand reaching

up to the door-knob, and the other throwing
disarming kisses to Samantha, — " By-by !
Lady Gay go circus now ! Timfy, come,
take Lady Gay to circus ! "

There was no time for discipline then,
and she was borne to the breakfast-table,
where Timothy was already making acquaintance with Miss Vilda.

Samantha entered, and Vilda, glancing
at her nervously, perceived with relief that
she was " taking things easy." Ah! but it
was lucky for poor David Milliken that he
could n't see her at that moment. Her
whole face had relaxed ; her mouth was no
longer a thin, hard line, but had a certain
curve and fullness, borrowed perhaps from
the warmth of innocent baby-kisses. Embarrassment and stifled joy had brought a
rosier color to her cheek ; Gay's vandal hand
had ruffled the smoothness of her sandy
locks, so that a few stray hairs were absolutely curling with amazement that they had
escaped from their sleek bondage ; in a word,
Samantha Ann Ripley was lovely and lovable !

Timothy had no eyes for any one save his
beloved Gay, at whom he gazed with unspeakable admiration, thinking it impossible

that any human being, with a single eye in its head, could refuse to take such an angel when it was in the market.

Gay, not being used to a regular morning toilet, had fought against it valiantly at first; but the tonic of the bath itself and the exercise of war had brought the color to her cheeks and the brightness to her eyes. She had forgiven Samantha, she was ready to be on good terms with Miss Vilda, she was at peace with all the world. That she was eating the bread of dependence did not trouble her in the least! No royal visitor, conveying honor by her mere presence, could have carried off a delicate situation with more distinguished grace and ease. She was perched on a Webster's Unabridged Dictionary, and immediately began blowing bubbles in her mug of milk in the most reprehensible fashion; and glancing up after each naughty effort with an irrepressible gurgle of laughter, in which she looked so bewitching, even with a milky crescent over her red mouth, that she would have melted the heart of the most predestinate old misogynist in Christendom.

Timothy was not so entirely at his ease. His eyes had looked into life only a few more summers, but their "radiant morning visions" had been dispelled; experience had tempered joy. Gay, however, had not arrived at an age where people's motives can be suspected for an instant. If there had been any possible plummet with which to sound the depths of her unconscious philosophy, she apparently looked upon herself as a guest out of heaven, flung down upon this hospitable planet with the single responsibility of enjoying its treasures.

O happy heart of childhood ! Your simple creed is rich in faith, and trust, and hope. You have not learned that the children of a common Father can do aught but love and help each other.

SCENE VIII.

The Old Garden.

"God Almighty first planted a garden, and it is indeed the purest of all human pleasures," said Lord Bacon, and Miss Vilda would have agreed with him. Her garden was not simply the purest of all her pleasures, it was her only one; and the love that other people gave to family, friends, or kindred she lavished on her posies.

It was a dear, old-fashioned, odorous garden, where Dame Nature had never been forced but only assisted to do her duty. Miss Vilda sowed her seeds in the springtime wherever there chanced to be room, and they came up and flourished and went to seed just as they liked, those being the only duties required of them. Two splendid groups of fringed "pinies," the pride of

Miss Avilda's heart, grew just inside the gate, and hard by the handsomest dahlias in the village, quilled beauties like carved rosettes of gold and coral and ivory. There was plenty of feathery "sparrowgrass," so handy to fill the black and yawning chasms of summer fireplaces and furnish green for "boquets." There was a stray peach or greengage tree here and there, and if a plain, well-meaning carrot chanced to lift its leaves among the poppies, why, they were all the children of the same mother, and Miss Vilda was not the woman to root out the invader and fling it into the ditch. There was a bed of yellow tomatoes, where, in the season, a hundred tiny golden balls hung among the green leaves; and just beside them, in friendly equality, a tangle of pink sweet-williams, fragrant phlox, delicate bride's-tears, canterbury bells blue as the June sky, none-so-pretties, gay cockscombs, and flaunting marigolds, which would insist on coming up all together, summer after summer, regardless of color harmonies. Last, but not least, there was a patch of sweet peas,

> "on tiptoe for a flight,
> With wings of gentle flush o'er delicate white."

These dispensed their sweet odors so gen-
erously that it was a favorite diversion
among the village children to stand in rows
outside the fence, and, elevating their bucolic
noses, simultaneously " sniff Miss Cummins'
peas." The garden was large enough to
have little hills and dales of its own, and
its banks sloped gently down to the river.
There was a gnarled apple tree hidden by
a luxuriant wild grapevine, a fit bower for
a " lov'd Celia " or a " fair Rosamond."
There was a spring, whose crystal waters
were " cabined, cribbed, confined " within
a barrel sunk in the earth ; a brook singing its way among the alder bushes, and
dripping here and there into pools, over
which the blue harebells leaned to see themselves. There was a summer-house, too, on
the brink of the hill ; a weather - stained
affair, with a hundred names carved on its
venerable lattices, — names of youths and
maidens who had stood there in the moonlight and plighted rustic vows.

If you care to feel a warm glow in the
region of your heart, imagine little Timothy
Jessup sent to play in that garden, — sent
to play for almost the first time in his life!
Imagine it, I ask, for there are some things

too sweet to prick with a pen-point.
Timothy stayed there fifteen minutes, and
running back to the house in a state of
intoxicated delight went up to Samantha, and
laying an insistent hand on hers said excitedly, " Oh, Samanthy, you did n't tell me —
there is shining water down in the garden;
not so big as the ocean, nor so still as the
harbor, but a kind of baby river running
along by itself with the sweetest noise.
Please, Miss Vilda, may I take Gay to see it,
and will it hurt it if I wash Rags in it?"

" Let 'em all go," suggested Samantha;
" there 's Jabe dawdlin' along the road, and
they might as well be out from under foot."

" Don't be too hard on Jabe this morning,
Samanthy, — he 's been to see the Baptist
minister at Edgewood; you know he 's going to be baptized some time next month."

" Well, he needs it! But land sakes!
you could n't make them Slocums pious 'f
you kep' on baptizin' of 'em till the crack
o' doom. I never hearn tell of a Slocum's
gittin' baptized in July. They allers take
'em after the freshets in the spring o' the
year, 'n' then they have to be turrible careful to douse 'em lengthways of the river.
Look at him, will ye? I b'lieve he 's

grown sence yesterday! If he 'd ever stood
stiff on his feet when he was a boy, he
need n't 'a' been so everlastin' tall; but he
was forever roostin' on fences' with his laigs
danglin', 'n' the heft of his feet stretched
'em out, — it could n't do no dif'rent. I
ain't got no patience with him."

"Jabe has considerable many good
points," said Miss Cummins loyally; "he 's
faithful, — you always know where to find
him."

"Good reason why," retorted Samantha.
"You always know where to find him 'cause
he gen'ally hain't moved sence you seen
him last. Gittin' religion ain't goin' to
help him much. If he ever hears tell 'bout
the gate of heaven bein' open 't the last day,
he won't 'a' begun to begin thinkin' 'bout
gittin' in tell he hears the door shet in his
face; 'n' then he 'll set ri' down 's comf'table 's if he was inside, 'n' say, 'Wall, better luck next time: slow an' sure 's my
motto!' Good-mornin', Jabe, — had your
dinner?"

"I ain't even hed my breakfast," responded Mr. Slocum easily.

"Blessed are the lazy folks, for they always git their chores done for 'em," re-

marked Samantha scathingly, as she went to
the buttery for provisions.

"Wall," said Laigs, looking at her with
his most irritating smile, as he sat down
at the kitchen table, "I don't find I git
thru any more work by tumblin' out o' bed
't sun-up 'n I dew 'f I lay a spell 'n' let
the univarse git het up 'n' runnin' a leetle
mite. 'Slow 'n' easy goes fur in a day' 's
my motto. Rhapseny, she used to say she
should think I 'd be ashamed to lay abed
so late. 'Wall, I be,' s' I, 'but I 'd ruther
be ashamed 'n git up!' But you 're an
awful good cook, Samanthy, if ye air allers
in a hurry, 'n' if yer hev got a sharp
tongue!"

"The less you say 'bout my tongue the
better!" snapped Samantha.

"Right you are," answered Jabe with a
good-natured grin, as he went on with his
breakfast. He had a huge appetite, another
grievance in Samantha's eyes. She always
said "there was no need of his being so slab-
sided 'n' slack-twisted 'n' knuckle-jointed,
— that he eat enough in all conscience, but
he would n't take the trouble to find the
victuals that would fat him up 'n' fill out
his bag o' bones."

Just as Samantha's well-cooked viands
began to disappear in Jabe's capacious
mouth (he always ate precisely as if he
were stoking an engine) his eye rested upon
a strange object by the wood-box, and he
put down his knife and ejaculated, " Well,
I swan! Now when 'n' where 'd I see that
baby-shay? Why, 't was yesterday. Well,
I vow, them young ones was comin' here,
was they ? "

" What young ones ? " asked Miss Vilda,
exchanging astonished glances with Samantha.

" And don't begin at the book o' Genesis
'n' go clean through the Bible, 's you gen-
'ally do. Start right in on Revelations,
where you belong," put in Samantha; for
to see a man unexpectedly loaded to the
muzzle with news, and too lazy to fire it off,
was enough to try the patience of a saint;
and even David Milliken would hardly have
applied that term to Samantha Ann Ripley.

" Give a feller time to think, will yer ? "
expostulated Jabe, with his mouth full of
pie. " Everything comes to him as waits 'd
be an awful good motto for you! Where 'd
I see 'em ? Why, I fetched 'em as fur as
the cross-roads myself."

" Well, I never ! " " I want to know ! "
cried the two women in one breath.

" I picked 'em up out on the road, a little
piece this side o' the station. 'T was at the
top o' Marm Berry's hill, that 's jest where
't was. The boy was trudgin' along draggin'
the baby 'n' the basket, 'n' I thought I 'd
give him a lift, so s' I, ' Goin' t' the Swamp
or t' the Falls?' s' I. ' To the Falls,' s' 'e.
' Git in,' s' I, ' 'n' I 'll give yer a ride, 'f y'
ain't in no hurry,' s' I. So in he got,
'n' the baby tew. When I got putty near
home, I happened ter think I 'd oughter
gone roun' by the tan'ry 'n' picked up the
Widder Foss, 'n' so s' I, ' I ain't goin'
no nearer to the Falls ; but I guess your
laigs is good for the balance o' the way,
ain't they?' s' I. ' I guess they be!' s' 'e.
Then he thanked me 's perlite 's Deacon
Sawyer's first wife, 'n' I left him 'n' his
folks in the road where I found 'em."

" Did n't you ask where he belonged nor
where he was bound ? "

" 'T ain't my way to waste good breath
askin' questions 't ain't none o' my bis'ness,"
replied Mr. Slocum.

" You 're right, it ain't," responded Samantha, as she slammed the milk-pans in

the sink; "'n' it's my hope that some time
when you get good and ready to ask somebody somethin' they'll be in too much of a
hurry to answer you!'"

"Be they any of your folks, Miss Vildy?"
asked Jabe, grinning with delight at Samantha's ill humor.

"No," she answered briefly.

"What yer cal'latin' ter do with 'em?"

"I haven't decided yet. The boy says
they haven't got any folks nor any home;
and I suppose it's our duty to find a place
for 'em. I don't see but we've got to go to
the expense of takin' 'em back to the city
and puttin' 'em in some asylum." ·

"How'd they happen to come here?"

"They ran away from the city yesterday,
and they liked the looks of this place; that's
all the satisfaction we can get out of 'em,
and I dare say it's a pack of lies."

"That boy wouldn't tell a lie no more 'n
a seraphim!" said Samantha tersely.

"You can't judge folks by appearances,"
answered Vilda. "But anyhow, don't talk `
to the neighbors, Jabe; and if you haven't
got anything special on hand to-day, I wish
you'd patch the roof of the summer house
and dig us a mess of beet greens. Keep

the children with you, and see what you
make of 'em; they 're playin' in the garden
now."

"All right. I 'll size 'em up the best I
ken, tho' mebbe it 'll hender me in my
work some; but time was made for slaves,
as the molasses said when they told it to
hurry up in winter time."

Two hours later, Miss Vilda looked from
the kitchen window and saw Jabez Slocum
coming across the road from the garden.
Timothy trudged beside him, carrying the
basket of greens in one hand, and the other
locked in Jabe's huge paw; his eyes up-
turned and shining with pleasure, his lips
moving as if he were chattering like a mag-
pie. Lady Gay was just where you might
have expected to find her, mounted on the
towering height of Jabe's shoulder, one tiny
hand grasping his weather-beaten straw hat,
while with the other she whisked her willing
steed with an alder switch which had evi-
dently been cut for that purpose by the vic-
tim himself.

"That 's the way he 's sizin' of 'em up,"
said Samantha, leaning over Vilda's shoulder
with a smile. "I 'll bet they 've sized him
up enough sight better 'n he has them!"

Jabe left the children outside, and came in with the basket. Putting his hat in the wood-box and hitching up his trousers impressively, he sat down on the settle.

"Them ain't no children to be wanderin' about the earth afoot 'n' alone, 'same 's Hitty went to the beach;' nor they ain't any common truck ter be put inter 'sylums 'n' poor-farms. There 's some young ones that 's so everlastin' chuckle-headed 'n' hombly 'n' contrairy that they ain't hardly wuth savin'; but these ain't that kind. The baby, now you 've got her cleaned up, is han'somer 'n any baby on the river, 'n' a reg'lar chunk o' sunshine besides. I 'd be willin' ter pay her a little suthin' for livin' alongside. The boy — well, the boy is a extra-ordinary boy. We got on tergether 's slick as if we was twins. That boy 's got idees, that 's what he 's got; 'n' he 's likely to grow up into — well, 'most anything."

"If you think so highly of 'em, why don't you adopt 'em?" asked Miss Vilda curtly. "That 's what they seem to think folks ought to do."

"I ain't sure but I shall," Mr. Slocum responded unexpectedly. "If you can't find a better home for 'em somewheres, I ain't

sure but I 'll take 'em myself. Land sakes!
if Rhapseny was alive I 'd adopt 'em quicker
'n blazes; but marm won't take to the idee
very strong, I don't s'pose, 'n' she ain't
much on bringin' up children, as I ken tes-
tify. Still, she 's a heap better 'n a brick asylum with a six-foot stone wall round it, when
yer come to that. But I b'lieve we ken do
better for 'em. I can say to folks, ' See here :
here 's a couple o' smart, han'some children.
You can have 'em for nothin', 'n' need n't
resk the onsartainty o' gittin' married 'n'
raisin' yer own; 'n' when yer come ter that,
yer would n't stan' no charnce o' gittin' any
as likely as these air, if ye did.' "

"That 's true as the gospel!" said Samantha. It nearly killed her to agree with him,
but the words were fairly wrung from her
unwilling lips by his eloquence and wisdom.

" Well, we 'll see what we can do for 'em,"
said Vilda in a non-committal tone; "and
here they 'll have to stay, for all I see, tell
we can get time to turn round and look 'em
up a place."

" And the way their edjercation has been
left be," continued Mr. Slocum, "is a burnin' shame in a Christian country. I don'
b'lieve they ever see the inside of a school-

house! I 've learned 'em more this mornin'
'n they ever hearn tell of before, but they 're
's ignorant 's Cooper's cow yit. They don'
know tansy from sorrel, nor slip'ry ellum
from pennyroyal, nor burdock from pig-
weed; they don' know a dand'lion from a
hole in the ground; they don' know where
the birds put up when it comes on night;
they never see a brook afore, nor a bull-frog;
they never hearn tell o' cat-o'-nine-tails, nor
jack-lanterns, nor see - saws. Land sakes!
we got ter talkin' 'bout so many things that
I clean forgot the summer-house roof. But
there! this won't do for me: I must be
goin'; there ain't no rest for the workin'-
man in this country."

"If there wa'n't no work for him, he 'd
be wuss off yet," responded, Samantha.

"Right ye are, Samanthy! Look here,
when 'd you want that box you give me to
fix?"

"I wanted it before hayin', but I s'pose
any time before Thanksgivin' 'll do, seein'
it 's you."

"What 's wuth doin' 't all 's wuth takin'
time over, 's my motto," said Jabe cheerfully, "but seein' it 's you, I 'll nail that
cover on ter night or bust!"

SCENE IX.

A Village Sabbath.

"NOW THE END OF THE COMMANDMENT IS
CHARITY, OUT OF A PURE HEART."

IT was Sunday morning, and the very
peace of God was brooding over Pleasant
River. Timothy, Rags, and Gay were play-
ing decorously in the orchard. Maria was
hitched to an apple-tree in the side yard,
and stood there serenely with her eyes half
closed, dreaming of oats past and oats to
come. Miss Vilda and Samantha issued
from the mosquito - netting door, clad in
Sunday best; and the children approached
nearer, that they might share in the excitement of the departure for " meeting." Gay
clamored to go, but was pacified by the gift
of a rag-doll that Samantha had made for
her the evening before. It was a mon-
strosity, but Gay dipped it instantly in the
alembic of her imagination, and it became a

beautiful, responsive little daughter, which she clasped close in her arms, and on which she showered the tenderest tokens of maternal affection.

Miss Vilda handed Timothy a little green-paper-covered book, before she climbed into the buggy. "That's a catechism," she said; "and if you'll be a good boy and learn the first six pages, and say 'em to me this afternoon, Samantha 'll give you a top that you can spin on week days."

"What is a catechism?" asked Timothy, as he took the book.

"It's a Sunday-school lesson."

"Oh, then I can learn it," said Timothy, brightening; "I learned three for Miss Dora, in the city."

"Well, I'm thankful to hear that you've had some spiritual advantages; now, stay right here in the orchard till Jabe comes; and don't set the house afire," she added, as Samantha took the reins and raised them for the mighty slap on Maria's back which was necessary to wake her from her Sunday slumber.

"Why would I want to set the house afire?" Timothy asked wonderingly.

"Well, I don't know 's you would want

to, but I thought you might get to playin'
with matches, though I 've hid 'em all."

"Play with matches!" exclaimed Timothy, in wide-eyed astonishment that a match
could appeal to anybody as a desirable plaything. "Oh, no, thank you; I should n't
have thought of it."

"I don't know as we ought to have left
'em alone," said Vilda, looking back, as Samantha urged the moderate Maria over the
road; "though I don't know exactly what
they could do."

"Except run away," said Samantha re-
flectively.

"I wish to the land they would! It
would be the easiest way out of a troublesome matter. Every day that goes by will
make it harder for us to decide what to do
with 'em; for you can't do by those you
know the same as if they were strangers."

There was a long main street running
through the village north and south. Toward the north it led through a sweet-scented
wood, where the grass tufts grew in verdant
strips along the little-traveled road. It had
been a damp morning, and, though now the
sun was shining brilliantly, the spiders' webs
still covered the fields; gossamer laces of

moist, spun silver, through which shone the pink and lilac of the meadow grasses. The wood was a quiet place, and more than once Miss Vilda and Samantha had discussed matters there which they would never have mentioned at the White Farm.

Maria went ambling along serenely through the arcade of trees, where the sun went wandering softly, " as with his hands before his eyes ; " overhead, the vast blue canopy of heaven, and under the trees the soft brown leaf carpet, "woven by a thousand autumns."

" I don't know but I could grow to like the baby in time," said Vilda, " though it 's my opinion she 's goin' to be dreadful troublesome ; but I 'm more 'n half afraid of the boy. Every time he looks at me with those searchin' eyes of his, I mistrust he 's goin' to say something about Marthy, — all on account of his giving me such a turn when he came to the door."

" He 'd be awful handy round the house, though, Vildy ; that is, if he *is* handy, — pickin' up chips, 'n' layin' fires, 'n' what not ; but, 's you say, he ain't so takin' as the baby at first sight. She 's got the same winnin' way with her that Marthy hed ! "

" Yes," said Miss Vilda grimly; " and I guess it 's the devil's own way."

" Well, yes, mebbe; 'n' then again mebbe 't ain't. There ain't no reason why the devil should own all the han'some faces 'n' tunesome laughs, 't I know of. It doos seem 's if beauty was turrible misleadin', 'n' I 've ben glad sometimes the Lord did n't resk none of it on me; for I was behind the door when good looks was give out, 'n' I 'm willin' t' own up to it; but, all the same, I like to see putty faces roun' me, 'n' I guess when the Lord sets his mind on it He can make goodness 'n' beauty git along comf'tably in the same body. When yer come to that, hombly folks ain't allers as good 's they might be, 'n' no comfort to anybody's eyes, nuther."

" You think the boy 's all right in the upper story, do you? He 's a strange kind of a child, to my thinkin'."

" I ain't so sure but he 's smarter 'n we be, but he talks queer, 'n' no mistake. This mornin' he was pullin' the husks off a baby ear o' corn that Jabe brought in, 'n' s' 'e, ' S'manthy, I think the corn must be the happiest of all the veg'tables.' ' How you talk!' s' I; ' what makes you think that way?'

'Why, because,' s' 'e, 'God has hidden it
away so safe, with all that shinin' silk round
it first, 'n' then the soft leaves wrapped outside o' the silk. I guess it's God's fav'rite
veg'table; don't you, S'manthy?' s' 'e. And
when I was showin' him pictures last night,
'n' he see the crosses on top some o' the city
meetin'-houses, s' 'e, 'They have two sticks
on 'most all the churches, don't they, S'manthy? I s'pose that's one stick for God, and
the other for the peoples.' Well, now, don't
you remember Seth Pennell, o' Buttertown,
how queer he was when he was a boy? We
thought he'd never be wuth his salt. He
used to stan' in the front winder 'n' twirl
the curtin tossel for hours to a time. And
don't you know it come out last year that
he'd wrote a reg'lar book, with covers on it
'n' all, 'n' that he got five dollars a colume
for writin' poetry verses for the papers?"

"Oh, well, if you mean that," said Vilda
argumentatively, "I don't call writin' poetry
any great test of smartness. There ain't
been a big fool in this village for years but
could do somethin' in the writin' line. I
guess it ain't any great trick, if you have a
mind to put yourself down to it. For my
part, I've always despised to see a great,

hulkin' man, that could handle a hoe or a
pitchfork, sit down and twirl a pen-stalk.''

" Well, I ain't so sure. I guess the Lord
hes his own way o' managin' things. We
ain't all cal'lated to hoe pertaters nor yet to
write poetry verses. There 's as much dif-
'rence in folks 's there is in anybody. Now,
I can take care of a dairy as well as the next
one, 'n' nobody was ever hearn to complain
o' my butter; but there was that lady in
New York State that used to make flowers
'n' fruit 'n' graven images out o' her churn-
in's. You 've hearn tell o' that piece she
carried to the Centennial? Now, no sech
doin's 's that ever come into my head. I 've
went on makin' round balls for twenty years ;
'n', massy on us, don't I remember when my
old butter stamp cracked, 'n' I could n't get
another with an ear o' corn on it, 'n' hed to
take one with a beehive, why, I was that
homesick I could n't bear to look my butter
'n the eye! But that woman would have
had a new picter on her balls every day,
I should n't wonder! (For massy's sake,
Maria, don't stan' stock still 'n' let the flies
eat yer right up!) No, I tell yer, it takes
all kinds o' folks to make a world. Now, I
could n't never read poetry. It 's so dull, it

makes me feel 's if I 'd been trottin' all day
in the sun! But there 's folks that can stan'
it, or they would n't keep on turnin' of it out.
The children are nice children enough, but
have they got any folks anywhere, 'n' what
kind of folks, 'n' where 'd they come from,
anyhow: that 's what we 've got to find out,
'n' I guess it 'll be consid'able of a chore!"

"I don't know but you 're right. I
thought some of sendin' Jabe to the city
to-morrow."

"Jabe? Well, I s'pose he 'd be back by
'nother spring; but who 'd we get ter shovel
us out this winter, seein' as there ain't more
'n three men in the whole village? Aunt
Hitty says twenty-year engagements 's goin'
out o' fashion in the big cities, 'n' I 'm glad
if they be. They 'd 'a' never come *in*, I told
her, if there 'd ever been an extry man in
these parts, but there never was. If you
got holt o' one by good luck, you had ter
keep holt, if 't was two years or twenty-two,
or go without. I used ter be too proud ter
go without; now I 've got more sense, thanks
be! Why don't you go to the city yourself, Vildy? Jabe Slocum ain't got sprawl
enough to find out anythin' wuth knowin'."

"I suppose I could go, though I don't

like the prospect of it very much. I have n't been there for years, but I 'd ought to look after my property there once in a while. Deary me! it seems as if we were n't ever going to have any more peace."

"Mebbe we ain't," said Samantha, as they wound up the meeting-house hill; "but ain't we hed 'bout enough peace for one spell? If peace was the best thing we could get in this world, we might as well be them old cows by the side o' the road there. There ain't nothin' so peaceful as a cow, when you come to that!"

The two women went into the church more perplexed in mind than they would have cared to confess. During the long prayer (the minister could talk to God at much greater length than he could talk about Him), Miss Vilda prayed that the Lord would provide the two little wanderers with some more suitable abiding-place than the White Farm; and that, failing this, He would inform his servant whether there was anything unchristian in sending them to a comfortable public asylum. She then re-minded Heaven that she had made the Foreign Missionary Society her residuary lega-tee (a deed that established her claim to being a zealous member of the fold), so that she could scarcely be blamed for not wishing to take two orphan children into her peaceful home.

Well, it is no great wonder that so faulty a prayer did not bring the wished-for light at once; but the ministering angels, who had the fatherless little ones in their care, did not allow Miss Vilda's mind to rest quietly. Just as the congregation settled itself after the hymn, and the palm-leaf fans began to sway in the air, a swallow flew in through the open window; and, after fluttering to and fro over the pulpit, hid itself in a dark corner, unnoticed by all save the small boys of the congregation, to whom it was, of course, a priceless boon. But Miss Vilda could not keep her wandering thoughts on the sermon any more than if she had been a small boy. She was anything but superstitious; but she had seen that swallow, or some of its ancestors, before. . . . It had flown into the church on the very Sunday of her mother's death. . . . They had left her sitting in the high-backed rocker by the window, the great family Bible and her spectacles on the little light-stand beside her. . . . When they returned from church, they had found their mother sitting as they left her, with a smile on her face, but silent and lifeless. . . . And through the glass of the spectacles, as they lay on the printed page, Vilda had read the words, " For a bird of the air shall carry the voice, and that which hath wings shall tell the matter; " had read them wonderingly, and marked the place with reverent fingers. . . . The swallow flew in again, years afterward. . . . She could not remember the day or the month, but she could never forget the summer, for it was the last bright one of her life, the last that pretty Martha ever spent at the White Farm. . . . And now here was the swallow again. . . . " For a bird of the air shall carry the voice, and that which hath wings shall tell the matter." Miss Vilda looked on the book and tried to follow the hymn; but passages of Scripture flocked into her head in place of good Dr. Watts's verses, and when the little melodeon played the interludes she could only hear : —

" Yea, the sparrow hath found her an house and the swallow a nest where she may lay her young, even Thy altars, O Lord of hosts, my King and my God."

" As a bird that wandereth from her nest, so is a man that wandereth from his place."

" The foxes have holes and the birds of the air have nests, but the Son of man hath not where to lay his head."

And then the text fell on her bewildered ears, and roused her from one reverie to plunge her in another. It was chosen, as it chanced, from the First Epistle of Timothy, chapter first, verse fifth: " Now the end of the commandment is charity, out of a pure heart."

" That means the Missionary Society," said Miss Vilda to her conscience, doggedly; but she knew better. The parson, the text, — or was it the bird? — had brought the message; but for the moment she did not lend the hearing ear or the understanding heart.

SCENE X.

The Supper Table.

AUNT HITTY COMES TO "MAKE OVER," AND SUP-
PLIES BACK NUMBERS TO ALL THE VILLAGE
HISTORIES.

AUNT HITTY, otherwise Mrs. Silas Tarbox, was as cheery and loquacious a person
as you could find in a Sabbath day's journey.
She was armed with a substantial amount of
knowledge at almost every conceivable point;
but if an unexpected emergency ever did
arise, her imagination was equal to the strain
put upon it and rose superior to the occasion.
Yet of an evening, or on Sunday, she was no
village gossip; it was only when you put a
needle in her hand or a cutting-board in her
lap that her memory started on its inter-
minable journeyings through the fields of
the past. She knew every biography and
every "ought-to-be-ography" in the county,
and could tell you the branches of every
genealogical tree in the village.

It was dusk at the White Farm, and a

late supper was spread upon the hospitable board. (Aunt Hitty was always sure of a bountiful repast. If one were going to economize, one would not choose for that purpose the day when the village seamstress came to sew; especially when the aforesaid lady served the community in the stead of a local newspaper.)

The children had eaten their bread and milk, and were out in the barn with Jabe, watching the milking. Aunt Hitty was in a cheerful mood as she reflected on her day's achievements. Out of Dr. Jonathan Cummins' old cape coat she had carved a pair of brief trousers and a vest for Timothy; out of Mrs. Jonathan Cummins' waterproof a serviceable jacket; and out of Deacon Abijah Cummins' linen duster an additional coat and vest for warm days. The owners of these garments had been dead many years, but nothing was ever thrown away (and, for that matter, very little given away) at the White Farm, and the ancient habiliments had finally been diverted to a useful purpose.

"I hope I shall relish my vittles to-night," said Aunt Hitty, as she poured her tea into her saucer, and set the cup in her little blue

"cup-plate;" " but I 've had the neura*l*gy so
in my face that 'it 's be'n more 'n ten days
sence I 've be'n able to carry a knife to my
mouth. . . . Your meat vittles is always so
tasty, Miss Cummins. I was sayin' to Mis'
Sawyer last week I think she lets her beef
hang too long. Its dretful tender, but I
don't b'lieve its hullsome. For my part, as
I 've many a time said to Si, I like meat with
some chaw to it. . . . Mis' Sawyer don't
put half enough vittles on her table. She
thinks it scares folks ; it don't me a mite, —
it makes me 's hungry as a wolf. When I
set a table for comp'ny I pile on a hull lot,
'n' I find it kind o' discourages 'em. . . .
Mis' Southwick 's hevin' a reg'lar brash o'
house-cleanin'. She 's too p'ison neat for
any earthly use, that woman is. She 's fixed
clam - shell borders roun' all her garding
beds, an' got enough left for a pile in one
corner, where she 's goin' to set her oleander
kag. Then she 's bought a haircloth chair
and got a new three-ply carpet in her parlor,
'n' put the old one in the spare-room 'n' the
back - entry. Her daughter 's down here
from New Haven. She 's married into one
of the first families o' Connecticut, Lobelia
has, 'n' she puts on a good many airs. She 's

rigged out her mother's parlor with lace cur-
tains 'n' one thing 'n' 'other, 'n' wants it
called the drawin'-room. Did ye ever hear
tell such foolishness? 'Drawin'-room!' s' I
to Si; 'what's it goin' to draw? Nothin'
but flies, I guess likely!' . . . Mis' Pennell's got a new girl to help round the
house, — one o' them pindlin' light-com-
plected Smith girls, from the Swamp, —
look's if they was nussed on bonny-clabber.
She's so hombly I sh'd think 't would make
her back ache to carry her head round. She
ain't very smart, neither. Her mother sent
word she'd pick up 'n' do better when she
got her growth. That made Mis' Pennell
hoppin' mad. She said she did n't cal'late
to pay a girl three shillin's a week for growin'. Mis' Pennell's be'n feelin' consid'able
slim, or she would n't 'a' hired help; it's
just like pullin' teeth for Deacon Pennell to
pay out money for anything like that. He
watches every mouthful the girl puts into
her mouth, 'n' it's made him 'bout down
sick to see her fleshin' up on his vittles. . . .
They say he has her put the mornin' coffee-
grown's to dry on the winder-sill, 'n' then
has 'em scalt over for dinner; but, there!
I don' know 's there's a mite o' truth in it,

so I won't repeat it. They went to him to
git a subscription for the new hearse the other
day. Land sakes! we need one bad enough.
I thought for sure, at the last funeral we
had, that they 'd never git Mis' Strout to the
graveyard safe and sound. I kep' a-thinkin'
all the way how she 'd 'a' took on, if she 'd
be'n alive. She was the most timersome woman 't ever was. She was a Thomson, 'n' all
the Thomsons was scairt at their own shad-
ders. Ivory Strout rid right behind the
hearse, 'n' he says his heart was in his mouth
the hull durin' time for fear 't would break
down. He did n't git much comfort out the
occasion, I guess! Wa'n't he mad he hed to
ride in the same buggy with his mother-in-
law! The minister planned it all out, 'n'
wrote down the order o' the mourners, 'n'
passeled him out with old Mis' Thomson. I
was stan'in' close by, 'n' I heard him say he
s'posed he could go that way if he must, but
't would spile the hull blamed thing for him!
. . . Well, as I was sayin', the seleckmen
went to Deacon Pennell to get a contribution
towards buyin' the new hearse; an' do you
know, he would n't give 'em a dollar? • He
told 'em he gave five dollars towards the
other one, twenty years ago, 'n' had n't never

got a cent's worth o' use out of it. That's
Deacon Pennell all over! As Si says, if the
grace o' God wa'n't given to all of us without money 'n' without price, you would n't
never hev ketched Deacon Pennell experi-
encin' religion! It's got to be a free gospel
't would convict him o' sin, that's certain!
. . . They say Seth Thatcher's married out
in Iowy. His mother's tickled 'most to
death. She heerd he was settin' up with a
girl out there, 'n' she was scairt to death for
fear he'd get served as Lemuel 'n' Cyrus
was. The Thatcher boys never hed any
luck gettin' married, 'n' they always took
disappointments in love turrible hard. You
know Cyrus set in that front winder o' Mis'
Thatcher's, 'n' rocked back 'n' forth for ten
year, till he wore out five cane-bottomed
cheers, 'n' then rocked clean through, down
cellar, all on account o' Crany Ann Sweat.
Well, I hope she got her comeuppance in
another world, — she never did in this; she
married well 'n' lived in Boston. . . . Mis'
Thatcher hopes Seth'll come home to live.
She's dretful lonesome in that big house, all
alone. She'd oughter have somebody for a
company-keeper. She can't see nothin' but
trees 'n' cows from her winders. . . . Beats

all, the places they used to put houses. . . .
Either they 'd get 'em right under foot so 't
you 'd most tread on 'em when you walked
along the road, or else they 'd set 'em clean
back in a lane, where the women folks
could n't see face o' clay week in 'n' week
out. . . .

"Joel Whitten's widder 's just drawed his
pension along o' his bein' in the war o' 1812.
. . . It 's took 'em all these years to fix it.
. . . Massy sakes! don't some folks have
their luck buttered in this world? . . . She
was his fourth wife, 'n' she never lived with
him but thirteen days 'fore he up 'n' died.
. . . It doos seem 's if the guv'ment might
look after things a little mite closer. . . .
Talk about Joel Whitten's bein' in the war
o' 1812! Everybody knows Joel Whitten
would n't have fit a skeeter! He never got
any further 'n Scratch Corner, any way, 'n'
there he clim a tree or hid behind a hen-
coop somewheres till the regiment got out o'
sight. . . . Yes: one, two, three, four, —
Huldy was his fourth wife. His first was a
Hogg, from Hoggses Mills. The second was
Dorcas Doolittle, aunt to Jabe Slocum ; she
did n't know enough to make soap, Dorcas
did n't. . . . Then there was Delia Weeks,

from the lower corner. . . . She did n't live
long. . . . There was somethin' wrong with
Delia. . . . She was one o' the thin-blooded,
white-livered kind. . . . You could n't get
her warm, no matter how hard you tried.
. . . She 'd set over a roarin' fire in the
cook-stove even in the prickliest o' the dog-
days. . . . The mill-folks used to say the
Whittens burnt more cut-roun's 'n' stick-
ens 'n any three fam'lies in the village.
. . . Well, after Delia died, then come
Huldy's turn, 'n' it 's she, after all, that 's
drawed the pension. . . . Huldy took Joel's
death consid'able hard, but I guess she 'll
perk up, now she 's come int' this money.
. . . She 's awful leaky-minded, Huldy is,
but she 's got tender feelin's. . . . One day
she happened in at noon-time, 'n' set down
to the table with Si 'n' I. . . . All of a suddent she bust right out cryin' when Si was
offerin' her a piece o' tripe, 'n' then it come
out that she could n't never bear the sight o'
tripe, it reminded her so of Joel! It seems
tripe was a favorite dish o' Joel's. All his
wives cooked it firstrate. . . . Jabe Slocum
seems to set consid'able store by them children, don't he ? . . . I guess he 'll never
ketch up with his work, now he 's got them

hangin' to his heels. . . . He doos beat all
for slowness! Slocum's a good name for
him, that's certain. An' 's if that wa'n't
enough, his mother was a Stillwell, 'n' her
mother was a Doolittle! . . . The Doolittles
was the slowest fam'ly in Lincoln County.
(Thank you, I'm well helped, Samanthy.)
Old Cyrus Doolittle was slower 'n a toad
funeral. He was a carpenter by trade, 'n'
he was twenty-five years buildin' his house;
'n' it warn't no great, either. . . . The
stagin' was up ten or fifteen years, 'n' he
shingled it four or five times before he got
roun', for one patch o' shingles used to wear
out 'fore he got the next patch on. He 'n'
Mis' Doolittle lived in two rooms in the L.
There was elegant banisters, but no stairs to
'em, 'n' no entry floors. There was a tiptop cellar, but there wa'n't no way o' gittin'
down to it, 'n' there wa'n't no conductors to
the cisterns. There was only one door panel
painted in the parlor. Land sakes! the
neighbors used to happen in 'bout every
week for years 'n' years, hopin' he'd get
another one finished up, but he never did, —
not to my knowledge. . . . Why, it's the
gospel truth that when Mis' Doolittle died
he had to have her embalmed, so 't he could

git the front door hung for the fun'ral!
(No more tea, I thank you; my cup ain't
out.) . . . Speakin' o' slow folks, Elder
Banks tells an awful good story 'bout Jabe
Slocum. . . . There's another man down
to Edgewood, Aaron Peek by name, that's
'bout as lazy as Jabe. An' one day, when
the loafers roun' the store was talkin' 'bout
'em, all of a suddent they see the two of 'em
startin' to come down Marm Berry's hill,
right in plain sight of the store. . . . Well,
one o' the Edgewood boys bate one o' the
Pleasant River boys that they could tell
which one of 'em was the laziest by the way
they come down that hill. . . . So they all
watched, 'n' bime by, when Jabe was most
down to the bottom of the hill, they was
struck all of a heap to see him break into a
kind of a jog trot 'n' run down the balance
o' the way. Well, then, they fell to quar-
relin'; for o' course the Pleasant River
folks said Aaron Peek was the laziest, 'n'
the Edgewood boys declared he hed n't got
no such record for laziness 's Jabe Slocum
hed; an' when they was explainin' of it, one
way 'n' 'nother, Elder Banks come along,
'n' they asked him to be the judge. When
he heerd tell how 't was, he said he agreed

with the Edgewood folks that Jabe was
lazier 'n Aaron. 'Well, I snum, I don't
see how you make that out,' says the Pleasant River boys; 'for Aaron walked down,
'n' Jabe run a piece o' the way.' 'If Jabe
Slocum run,' says the elder, as impressive as
if he was preachin', — 'if Jabe Slocum ever
run, then 't was because he was *too doggoned
lazy to hold back!*' an' that settled it!. . .
(No, I could n't eat another mossel, Miss
Cummins; I've made out a splendid supper.)
. . . You can't git such pie 'n' doughnuts
anywhere else in the village, 'n' what I say
I mean. . . . Do you make your riz doughnuts with emptin's? I want to know! Si
says there's more faculty in cookin' flour
food than there is in meat-victuals, 'n' I
guess he's 'bout right."

. . . .

It was bedtime, and Timothy was in his
little room carrying on the most elaborate
and complicated plots for reading the future.
It must be known that Jabe Slocum was as
full of signs as a Farmer's Almanac, and he
had given Timothy more than one formula
for attaining his secret desires, — old, well-
worn recipes for luck, which had been tried
for generations in Pleasant River, and which

were absolutely " certain " in their results.
The favorites were : —

" Star bright, star light,
First star I 've seen to-night,
Wish I may, wish I might,
Get the wish I wish to-night ; "

and one still more impressive : —

" Four posts upon my bed,
Four corners overhead ;
Matthew, Mark, Luke, and John,
Bless the bed I *lay* upon.
Matthew, John, Luke, and Mark,
Grant my wish and keep it dark."

These rhymes had been chanted with
great solemnity, and Timothy sat by the
open window in the sweet darkness of the
summer night, wishing that he and Gay
might stay forever in this sheltered spot.
" I 'll make a sign of my very own," he
thought. " I 'll get Gay's ankle-tie, and put
it on the window-sill, with the toe pointing
out. Then I 'll wish that if we are going
to stay at the White Farm, the angels will
turn it around, ' toe in ' to the room, for a
sign to me ; and if we 've got to go, I 'll
wish they may leave it the other way ; and,
oh dear, but I 'm glad it 's so little and easy
to move ; and then I 'll say Matthew, Mark,
Luke, and John, four times over, without

stopping, as Jabe told me to, and then see how it turns out in the morning." . . .

But the incantation was more soothing than the breath of Miss Vilda's scarlet poppies, and before the magical verse had fallen upon the drowsy air for the third time, Timothy was fast asleep, with a smile of hope on his parted lips.

There was a sweet summer shower in the night. The soft breezes, fresh from shaded dells and nooks of fern, fragrant with the odor of pine and vine and wet wood-violets, blew over the thirsty meadows and golden stubble-fields, and brought an hour of gentle rain.

It sounded a merry tintinnabulation on Samantha's milk-pans, wafted the scent of dripping honeysuckle into the farmhouse windows, and drenched the night-caps in which prudent farmers had dressed their haycocks.

Next morning, the green world stood on tiptoe to welcome the victorious sun, and every little leaf shone as a child's eyes might shine at the remembrance of a joy just past.

A meadow lark perched on a swaying apple-branch above Martha's grave, and poured out his soul in grateful melody; and

Timothy, wakened by Nature's sweet good-morning, leaped from the too fond embrace of Miss Vilda's feather-bed. . . . And lo, a miracle! . . . The woodbine clung close to the wall beneath his window. It was tipped with strong young shoots reaching out their innocent hands to cling to any support that offered ; and one baby tendril that seemed to have grown in a single night, so delicate it was, had somehow been blown by the sweet night wind from its drooping place on the parent vine, and, falling on the window-sill, had curled lovingly round Gay's fairy shoe, and held it fast!

SCENE XI.

The Honeysuckle Porch.

MISS VILDA DECIDES THAT TWO IS ONE TOO
MANY, AND TIMOTHY BREAKS A HUMMING-
BIRD'S EGG.

IT was a drowsy afternoon. The grasshoppers chirped lazily in the warm grasses,
and the toads blinked sleepily under the
shadows of the steps, scarcely snapping at
the flies as they danced by on silver wings.
Down in the old garden the still pools, in
which the laughing brook rested itself here
and there, shone like glass under the strong
beams of the sun, and the baby horned-
pouts rustled their whiskers drowsily and
scarcely stirred the water as they glided
slowly through its crystal depths.

The air was fragrant with the odor of
new-mown grass and the breath of wild
strawberries that had fallen under the sickle,
to make the sweet hay sweeter with their
crimson juices. The whir of the scythes

and the clatter of the mowing machine came
from the distant meadows. Field mice and
ground sparrows were aware that it probably was all up with their little summer resi-
dences, for haying time was at its height,
and the Giant, mounted on the Avenging
Chariot, would speedily make his appear-
ance, and buttercups and daisies, tufted
grasses and blossoming weeds, must all bow
their heads before him, and if there was anything more valuable hidden at their roots,
so much the worse !

And if a bird or a mouse had been especially far-sighted and had located his family near a stump fence on a particularly un-
even bit of ground, why there was always a
walking Giant going about the edges with a
gleaming scythe, so that it was no wonder,
when reflecting on these matters after a
day's palpitation, that the little denizens of
the fields thought it very natural that there
should be Nihilists and Socialists in the
world, plotting to overturn monopolies and
other gigantic schemes for crushing the
people.

Rags enjoyed the excitement of haying
immensely. But then, his life was one long
holiday now anyway, and the close quarters,

scanty fare, and wearisome monotony of
Minerva Court only visited his memory
dimly when he was suffering the pangs of
indigestion.   For in the first few weeks of
his life at the White Farm, before his appetite was satiated, he was wont to eat all
the white cat's food as well as his own ; and
as this highway robbery took place in the
retirement of the shed, where Samantha
Ann always swept them for their meals, no
human being was any the wiser, and only
the angels saw the white cat getting whiter
and whiter and thinner and thinner, while
every day Rags grew more corpulent and
aldermanic in his figure.   But as his stomach was more favorably located than an
alderman's, he could still see the surround-
ing country, and he had the further advan-
tage of possessing four legs (instead of two)
to carry it about.

Timothy was happy, too, for he was a
dreamer, and this quiet life harmonized well
with the airy fabric of his dreams.   He
loved every stick and stone about the old
homestead already, because the place had
brought him the only glimpse of freedom
and joy that he could remember in these
last bare and anxious years ; and if there

were other and brighter years, far, far back
in the misty gardens of the past, they only
yielded him a secret sense of "having
been," a memory that could never be cap-
tured and put into words.

Each morning he woke fearing to find his
present life a vision, and each morning he
gazed with unspeakable gladness at the
sweet reality that stretched itself before his
eyes as he stood for a moment at his little
window above the honeysuckle porch.

There were the cucumber frames (he
had helped Jabe to make them); the old
summer house in the garden (he had held
the basket of nails and handed Jabe the
tools when he patched the roof); the little
workshop where Samantha potted her tomato
plants (and he had been allowed to water
them twice, with fingers trembling at the
thought of too little or too much for the tender things); and the grindstone where Jabe
ground the scythes and told him stories as
he sat and turned the wheel, while Gay sat
beside them making dandelion chains. Yes,
it was all there, and he was a part of it.

Timothy had all the poet's faculty of in-
terpreting the secrets that are hidden in
every-day things, and when he lay prone on

the warm earth in the cornfield, deep among
the "varnished crispness of the jointed
stalks," the rustling of the green things
growing sent thrills of joy along the sensitive currents of his being. He was busy in
his room this afternoon putting little parti-
tions in some cigar boxes, where, very soon,
two or three dozen birds' eggs were to re-
pose in fleece-lined nooks : for Jabe Slocum's collection of three summers (every
egg acquired in the most honorable manner,
as he explained), had all passed into Timothy's hands that very day, in consideration
of various services well and conscientiously
performed. What a delight it was to handle the precious bits of things, like porcelain
in their daintiness! — to sort out the tender
blue of the robin, the speckled beauty of
the sparrow; to put the pee-wee's and the
thrush's each in its place, with a swift throb
of regret that there would have been another little soft throat bursting with a song,
if some one had not taken this pretty egg.
And there was, over and above all, the
never ending marvel of the one humming-
bird's egg that lay like a pearl in Timothy's
slender brown hand. Too tiny to be stroked
like the others, only big enough to be stealth

ily kissed. So tiny that he must get out of bed two or three times in the night to see if it is safe. So tiny that he has horrible fears lest it should slip out or be stolen, and so he must take the box to the window and let the moonlight shine upon the fleecy cotton, and find that it is still there, and cover it safely over again and creep back to bed, wishing that he might see a "thumb's bigness of burnished plumage" sheltering it with her speck of a breast. Ah! to have a little humming-bird's egg to love, and to feel that it was his very own, was something to Timothy, as it is to all starved human hearts full of love that can find no outlet.

Miss Vilda was knitting, and Samantha was shelling peas, on the honeysuckle porch. It had been several days since Miss Cummins had gone to the city, and had come back no wiser than she went, save that she, had made a somewhat exhaustive study of the slums, and had acquired a more intimate knowledge of the ways of the world than she had ever possessed before. She had found Minerva Court, and designated it on her return as a "sink of iniquity," to which Afric's sunny fountains, India's coral strand, and other tropical localities frequented by missionaries were virtuous in comparison.

"For you don't expect anything of black heathens," said she; "but there ain't any question in my mind about the accountability of folks livin' in a Christian country, where you can wear clothes and set up to an air-tight stove and be comfortable, to say nothin' of meetin'-houses every mile or two, and Bible Societies and Young Men's and Young Women's Christian Associations, and the gospel free to all with the exception of pew rents and contribution boxes, and those omitted when it's necessary."

She affirmed that the ladies and gentlemen whose acquaintance she had made in Minerva Court were, without exception, a "mess of malefactors," whose only good point was that, lacking all human qualities, they did n't care who she was, nor where she came from, nor what she came for; so that as a matter of fact she had escaped without so much as leaving her name and place of residence. She learned that Mrs. Nancy Simmons had sought pastures new in Montana; that Miss Ethel Montmorency still resided in the metropolis, but did not choose to disclose her modest dwelling-place

to the casual inquiring female from the ru-
ral districts; that a couple of children had
disappeared from Minerva Court, if they remembered rightly, but that there was no dis-
turbance made about the matter as it saved
several people much trouble; that Mrs. Morrison had had no relations, though she possessed a large circle of admiring friends;
that none of the admiring friends had called
since her death or asked about the children;
and finally that Number 3 had been turned
into a saloon, and she was welcome to go in
and slake her thirst for information with
something more satisfactory than she could·
get outside.

The last straw, and one that would have
broken the back of any self-respecting (unmarried) camel in the universe, was the of-
fensive belief, on the part of the Minerva
Courtiers, that the rigid Puritan maiden
who was conducting the examination was
the erring mother of the children, visiting
(in disguise) their former dwelling-place.
The conversation on this point becoming ex-
tremely pointed and jocose, Miss Cummins
finally turned and fled, escaping to the railway station as fast as her trembling legs
could carry her. So the trip was a fruitless

one, and the mystery that enshrouded Timothy and Lady Gay was as impenetrable as ever.

"I wish I 'd 'a' gone to the city with you," remarked Samantha. "Not that I could 'a' found out anything more 'n you did, for I guess there ain't anybody thereabouts that knows more 'n we do, and anybody 't wants the children won't be troubled with the relation. But I 'd like to give them bold-faced jigs 'n' hussies a good piece o' my mind for once! You 're too timersome, Vildy! I b'lieve I 'll go some o' these days yet, and carry a good stout umbrella in my hand too. It says in a book somewhar's that there 's insults that can only be wiped out in blood. Ketch 'em hintin' that I 'm the mother of anybody, that 's all! I declare I don' know what our Home Missionary Societies 's doin' not to regenerate them places or exterminate 'em, one or t' other. Somehow our religion don't take holt as it ought to. It takes a burnin' zeal to clean out them slum places, and burnin' zeal ain't the style nowadays. As my father used to say, 'Religion 's putty much like fish 'n' pertetters; if it 's hot it 's good, 'n' if it 's cold 'tain't wuth a ' — well, a short word come in

there, but I won't say it. Speakin' o' religion, I never had any experience in teachin',
but I did n't s'pose there was any knack
'bout teachin' religion, same as there is
'bout teachin' readin' 'n' 'rithmetic, but I
hed hard work makin' Timothy understand
that catechism you give him to learn the
other Sunday. He was all upsot with doctrine when he come to say his lesson. Now
you can't scare some children with doctrine,
no matter how hot you make it, or mebbe
they don't more 'n half believe it; but
Timothy 's an awful sensitive creeter, 'n'
when he come to that answer to the question
' What are you then by nature? An enemy
to God, a child of Satan, and an heir of hell,'
he hid his head on my shoulder and bust
right out cryin'. ' How many Gods is
there?' s ' e, after a spell. ' Land!' thinks
I, ' I knew he was a heathen, but if he turns
out to be an idolater, whatever shall I do
with him!' ' Why, where 've you ben fetched
up?' s' I. ' There 's only one God, the High
and Mighty Ruler of the Univarse,' s' I.
' Well,' s ' e', ' there must be more 'n one, for
the God in this lesson is n't like the one in
Miss Dora's book at all!' Land sakes! I
don't want to teach catechism agin in a

hurry, not tell I 've hed a little spiritual in-
struction from the minister. The fact is,
Vildy, that our b'liefs, when they 're picked
out o' the Bible and set down square and
solid 'thout any softening down 'n' explainin' that they ain't so bad as they sound,
is too strong meat for babes. Now I 'm
Orthodox to the core" (here she lowered
her voice as if there might be a stray
deacon in the garden), "but 'pears to me if
I was makin' out lessons for young ones I
would n't fill 'em so plumb full o' brimstun.
Let 'em do a little suthin' to deserve it 'fore
you scare 'em to death, say I."

"Jabe explained it all out to him after
supper. It beats all how he gets on with
children."

"I 'd ruther hear how he explained it,"
answered Samantha sarcastically. "He 's
great on expoundin' the Scripters jest now.
Well, I hope it 'll last. Land sakes! you 'd
think nobody ever experienced religion afore,
he 's so set up 'bout it. You 'd s'pose he
kep' the latch-key o' the heavenly mansions
right in his vest pocket, to hear him go on.
He could n't be no more stuck up 'bout it if
he 'd ben one o' the two brothers that come
over in three ships!"

"There goes Elder Nichols," said Miss Vilda. "Now there's a plan we had n't thought of. We might take the children over to Purity Village. I think likely the Shakers would take 'em. They like to get young folks and break 'em into their doctrines."

"Tim 'd make a tiptop Shaker," laughed Samantha. "He 'd be an Elder afore he was twenty - one. I can seem to see him now, with his hair danglin' long in his neck, a blue coat buttoned up to his chin, and his hands see-sawin' up 'n' down, prancin' round in them solemn dances."

"Tim would do well enough, but I ain't so sure of Gay. They 'd have their hands full, I guess!"

"I guess they would. Anybody that wanted to make a Shaker out o' her would 'a' had to begin with her grandmother; and that would n't 'a' done nuther, for they don't b'lieve in marryin', and the thing would 'a' stopped right there, and Gay would n't never 'a' been born int' the world."

"And been a great sight better off," interpolated Miss Vilda.

"Now don't talk that way, Vildy. Who

knows what lays ahead o' that child? The
Lord may be savin' her up to do some great
work for Him," she added, with a wild
flight of the imagination.

"She looks like it, don't she?" asked
Vilda with a grim intonation; but her face
softened a little as she glanced at Gay
asleep on the rustic bench under the window.

The picture would have struck terror to
the sad-eyed æsthete, but an artist who liked
to see colors burn and glow on the canvas
would have been glad to paint her: a little frock of buttercup yellow calico, bare
neck and arms, full of dimples, hair that
put the yellow calico to shame by reason of
its tinge of copper, skin of roses and milk
that dared the microscope, red smiling lips,
one stocking and ankle-tie kicked off and
five pink toes calling for some silly woman
to say "This little pig went to market" on
them, a great bunch of nasturtiums in one
warm hand and the other buried in Rags,
who was bursting with the white cat's dinner, and in such a state of snoring bliss
that his tail wagged occasionally, even in his
dreams.

"She don't look like a missionary, if that's

what you mean," said Samantha hotly. "She
may not be called 'n' elected to traipse over
to Africy with a Test'ment in one hand 'n'
a sun umbreller in the other, savin' souls
by the wholesale; but 't ain't no mean service to go through the world stealin' into
folks' hearts like a ray o' sunshine, 'n' lightin' up every place you step foot in!'"

"I ain't sayin' anything against the child,
Samanthy Ann; you said yourself she wa'n't
cut out for a Shaker!"

"No more she is," laughed Samantha,
when her good humor was restored. "She 'd
like the singin' 'n' dancin' well enough,
but 't would be hard work smoothin' the
kink out of her hair 'n' fixin' it under
one o' their white Sunday bunnets. She
would n't like livin' altogether with the
women-folks, nuther. The only way for
Gay 'll be to fetch her right up with the
men-folks, 'n' hev her see they ain't no great
things, anyway. Land sakes! If 't warn't
for dogs 'n' dark nights, I should n't care if
I never see a man; but Gay has 'em all on
her string a'ready, from the boy that brings
the cows home for Jabe to the man that
takes the butter to the city. The tin ped-
dler give her a dipper this mornin', and the

fish-man brought her a live fish in a tin pail. Well, she makes the house a great sight brighter to live in, you can't deny that, Vildy."

"I ain't denyin' anything in partic'ler. She makes a good deal of work, I know that much. And I don't want you to get your heart set on one or both of 'em, for 't won't be no use. We could make out with one of 'em, I suppose, if we had to, but two is one too many. They seem to set such store by one another that 't would be like partin' the Siamese twins; but there, they 'd pine awhile, and then they 'd get over it. Anyhow, they 'll have to try."

"Oh yes; you can git over the small-pox, but you 'll carry the scars to your grave most likely. I think 't would be a sin to part them children. I would n't do it no more 'n I 'd tear away that scarlit bean that 's twisted itself round 'n' round that pink hollyhock there. I stuck a stick in the ground, and carried a string to the winder; but I did n't git at it soon enough, the bean vine kep' on growin' the other way, towards the hollyhock. Then the other night I got my mad up, 'n' I jest oncurled it by main force 'n' wropped it round the

string, 'n,' if you 'll believe me, I happened
to look at it this mornin',' 'n' there it 't was,
as nippant as you please, coiled round the
hollyhock agin! Then says I to myself,
'Samantha Ann Ripley, you 've known what
't was to be everlastin'ly hectored 'n' intefered with all your life, now s'posin' you let
that bean have its hollyhock, if it wants it!'"

Miss Vilda looked at her sharply as she
said, "Samantha Ann Ripley, I believe to
my soul you 're fussin' 'bout Dave Milliken
again!"

"Well, I ain't! Every time I talk 'bout
hollyhocks and scarlit beans I ain't meanin'
Dave Milliken 'n' me, — not by a long
chalk! I was only givin' you my views
'bout partin' them children, that 's all!"

"Well, all I can say is," remarked Miss
Vilda obstinately, "that those that 's desir-
ous of takin' in two strange children, and
boardin' and lodgin' 'em till they get able
to do it for themselves, and runnin' the resk
of their turnin' out heathens and malefactors like the folks they came from, — can
do it if they want to. If I come to see that
the baby is too young to send away anywheres I may keep her a spell, but the boy
has got to go, and that 's the end of it.

You 've been crowdin' me into a corner about him for a week, and now I 've said my say ! "

Alas! that tiny humming-bird's egg was crushed to atoms, — crushed by a boy's slender hand that had held it so gently for very fear of breaking it. For poor little Timothy Jessup had heard his fate for the second time, and knew that he must "move on " again, for there was no room for him at the White Farm.

SCENE XII.

The Village.

LYDDY PETTIGROVE'S FUNERAL.

LYDDY PETTIGROVE was dead. Not one person, but a dozen, had called in at the White Farm to announce this fact and look curiously at Samantha Ann Ripley to see how she took the news.

To say the truth, the community did not seem to be overpowered by its bereavement. There seemed to be a general feeling that Mrs. Pettigrove had never been wanted in Pleasant River, coupled with a mild surprise that she should have been wanted anywhere else. Speculation was rife as to who would keep house for Dave Milliken, and whether Samantha Ann would bury the Ripley-Milliken battle-axe and go to the funeral, and whether Mis' Pettigrove had left her property to David, as was right, or to her husband's sister in New Hampshire, which would be a sin and a shame; but jest as

likely as not, though she was well off and
did n't need it no more 'n a toad would a
pocket-book, and could n't bear the sight o'
Lyddy besides, — and whether Mr. 'Pettigrove's first wife's relations would be asked
to the funeral, bein' as how they had n't
spoke for years, 'n' would n't set on the same
side the meetin'-house, but when you come
to that, if only the folks that was on good
terms with Lyddy Pettigrove was asked to
the funeral, there 'd be a slim attendance,
and — so on.

Aunt Hitty was the most important person in the village on these occasions. It
was she who assisted in the last solemn
preparations and took the last solemn
stitches; and when all was done, and she
hung her little reticule on her arm, and
started to walk from the house of bereavement to her own home (where "Si" was
anxiously awaiting his nightly draught of
gossip), no royal herald could have been
looked for with greater interest or greeted
with greater cordiality. All the housewives
that lived on the direct road were on their
doorsteps, so as not to lose a moment, and
all that lived off the road had seen her from
the upstairs windows, and were at the gate

to waylay her as she passed. At such a moment Aunt Hitty's bosom swelled with honest pride, and she humbly thanked her Maker that she had been bred to the use of scissors and needle.

Two days of this intoxicating popularity had just passed ; the funeral was over, and she ran in to the White Farm on her way home, to carry a message, and to see with her own eyes how Samantha Ann Ripley was comporting herself.

" You did n't git out to the fun'ral, did ye, Samanthy ? " she asked, as she seated herself cosily by the kitchen window.

" No, I did n't. I never could see the propriety o' goin' to see folks dead that you never went to see alive."

" How you talk ! That 's one way o' puttin' it ! Well, everybody was lookin' for you, and you missed a very pleasant fun'ral. David 'n' I arranged everything as neat as wax, and it all went off like clock-work, if I do say so as should n't. Mis' Pettigrove made a beautiful remains."

" I 'm glad to hear it. It 's the first beautiful thing she ever did make, I guess ! "

" How you talk ! Ain't you a leetle hard on Lyddy, Samanthy ? She warn't sech a bad neighbor, and she could n't help bein' kind o' sour like. She was born with her teeth on aidge, to begin with, and then she 'd ben through seas o' trouble with them Pettigroves."

" Like enough; but even if folks has ben through seas o' trouble, they need n't be everlastin'ly spittin' up salt brine. 'Passin' through the valley of sorrow they make it full o' fountings;' that 's what the Psalms says 'bout bearin' trouble."

" Lyddy warn't much on fountings," said Aunt Hitty contemplatively; " but, there, we had n't ought to speak nothin' but good o' the dead. Land sakes! You 'd oughter heard Elder Weekses remarks; they was splendid. We ain't hed better remarks to any fun'ral here for years. I should n't 'a' suspicioned he was preachin' 'bout Lyddy, though. Our minister 's sick abed, you know, 'n' warn't able to conduct the ex'cises. Si thinks he went to bed a-purpose, but I would n't hev it repeated; so David got Elder Weeks from Moderation. He warn't much acquainted with the remains, but he done all the better for that. He 's got a wond'ful faculty for fun'rals. They say he 's sent for for miles around. He 'd just

come from a fun'ral nine miles the other
side o' Moderation, up on the Blueb'ry road;
so he was a leetle mite late, 'n' David 'n' I
was as nervous as witches, for every room
was cram full 'n' the thermometer stood at
87 in the front entry, 'n' the bearers sot out
there by the well-curb, with the sun beatin'
down on 'em, 'n' two of 'em, Squire Hicks
'n' Deacon Dunn, was fast asleep. Inside,
everything was as silent 's the tomb, 'cept
the kitchen clock, 'n' that ticked loud enough
to wake the dead most. I thought I should
go inter conniptions. I set out to git up 'n'
throw a shawl over it, it ticked so loud.
Then, while we was all settin' there 's solemn 's the last trump, what does old Aunt
Beccy Burnham do but git up from the
kitchen corner where she sot, take the corn-
broom from behind the door, and sweep
down a cobweb that was lodged up in one
o' the corners over the mantelpiece! We
all looked at one 'nother, 'n' I thought for
a second somebody 'd laugh, but nobody
dassed, 'n' there warn't a sound in the room
's Aunt Beccy sot down agin' without movin' a muscle in her face. Just then the minister drove in the yard with his horse sweat-
in' like rain; but behind time as he was, he

never slighted things a mite. His prayer was twenty - three minutes by the clock. Twenty-three minutes is a leetle mite too long this kind o' weather, but it was an all-embracin' prayer, 'n' no mistake! Si said when he got through the Lord had his instructions on most any p'int that was likely to come up durin' the season. When he got through his remarks there warn't a dry eye in the room. I don't s'pose it made any odds whether he was preachin' 'bout Mis' Pettigrove or the woman on the Blueb'ry road, — it was a movin', elevatin' discourse, 'n' that was what we went there for."

"It would n't 'a' ben so elevatin' if he 'd told the truth," said Samantha; "but, there, I ain't goin' to spit no more spite out. Lyddy Pettigrove 's dead, 'n' I hope she 's in heaven, and all I can say is, that she 'll be dretful busy up there ondoin' all she done down here. You say there was a good many out?"

"Yes; we ain't hed so many out for years, so Susanna Rideout says, and she 'd ought to know, for she ain't missed a fun'ral sence she was nine years old, and she 's eighty-one, come Thanksgivin', ef she holds out that long. She says fun'rals is 'bout the only

recreation she has, 'n' she doos git a heap
o' satisfaction out of 'em, 'n' no mistake.
She'll go early, afore any o' the comp'ny as-
sembles. She'll say her clock must 'a' ben
fast, 'n' then they'll ask her to set down 'n'
make herself to home. Then she'll choose
her seat accordin' to the way the house is
planned. She won't git too fur from the
remains, because she'll want to see how the
fam'ly appear when they take their last look,
but she'll want to git opp'site a door, where
she can look into the other rooms 'n' see
whether they shed any tears when the minister begins his remarks. She allers takes
a little gum camphire in her pocket, so 't if
anybody faints away durin' the long prayer,
she's right on hand. Bein' near the door,
she can hear all the minister says, 'n' how
the order o' the mourners is called, 'n' ef
she ain't too fur from the front winders she
can hev a good view of the bearers and the
mourners as they get into the kerridges.
There's a sight in knowin' how to manage
at a fun'ral; it takes faculty, same as anything else."

"How does David bear up?" asked Miss
Vilda.

"Oh, he's calm. David was always calm

and resigned, you know. He shed tears durin' the remarks, but I s'pose, mebbe, he was wishin' they was more appropriate. He's about the forlornest creeter now you ever see in your life. There never was any self-assume to David Milliken. I declare it's enough to make you cry jest to look at him. I cooked up victuals enough to last him a week, but that ain't no way for menfolks to live. When he comes in at noontime he washes up out by the pump, 'n' then he steps int' the butt'ry 'n' pours some cold tea out the teapot 'n' takes a drink of it, 'n' then a bite o' cold punkin pie 'n' then more tea, all the time stan'in' up to the shelf 'stid o' sittin' down like a Christian, and lookin' out the winder as if his mind was in Hard Scrabble 'n' his body in Buttertown, 'n' as if he did n't know whether he was eatin' pie or putty. Land! I can't bear to watch him. I dassay he misses Lyddy's jawin', —it must seem dretful quiet. I declare it seems to me that meek, resigned folks, that's too good to squeal out when they're abused, is allers the ones that gits the hardest knocks; but I don't doubt but what there's goin' to be an everlastin' evenupness somewheres."

Samantha got up suddenly and went to the sink window. "It's 'bout time the men come in for their dinner," she said. But though Jabe was mowing the millstone hill, and though he wore a red flannel shirt, she could not see him because of the tears that blinded her eyes.

SCENE XIII.

The Village.

PLEASANT RIVER IS BAPTIZED WITH THE SPIRIT OF ADOPTION.

" BUT I did n't come in to talk 'bout the fun'ral," continued Aunt Hitty, wishing that human flesh were transparent so that she could see through Samanthy Ann Ripley's back. "I had an errant 'n' oughter ben in afore, but I 've ben so busy these last few days I could n't find rest for the sole o' my foot skersely. I 've sewed in seven dif'rent houses sence I was here last, and I 've made it my biz'ness to try 'n' stop the gossip 'bout them children 'n' give folks the rights o' the matter, 'n' git 'em int'rested to do somethin' for 'em. Now there ain't a livin' soul that wants the boy, but " —

"Timothy," said Miss Vilda hurriedly, "run and fetch me a passle of chips, that 's a good boy. Land sakes! Aunt Hitty, you need n't tell him to his face that nobody

wants him. He's got feelin's like any other
child."

"He set there so quiet with a book in
front of him I clean forgot he was in the
room," said Aunt Hitty apologetically.
"Land! I'm so tender-hearted I can't set
my foot on a June bug 'n' 't aint' likely I'd
hurt anybody's feelin's, but as I was sayin'
I can't find nobody that wants the boy, but
the Doctor's wife thinks p'raps she'll be willin' to take the baby 'n' board her for nothin', if somebody else 'll pay for her clothes.
At least she 'll try her a spell 'n' see how she
behaves, 'n' whether she 's good comp'ny for
her own little girl that 's a reg'lar limb o'
Satan anyway, 'n' consid'able worse sence
she 's had the scarlit fever, 'n' deef as a post
too, tho' they 're blisterin' her, 'n' she may
git over it. I told her I 'd bring Gay over
to-night as I was comin' by, bein' as how she
was worn out with sickness 'n' house-cleanin'
'n' one thing 'n' nother, 'n' could n't come to
git her very well herself. I thought mebbe
you 'd be willin' to pay for her clothes ruther
'n hev so much talk 'bout it, tho' I 've told
everybody that they walked right in to the
front gate, 'n' you 'n' Samanthy never set
eyes on 'em before, 'n' did n't know where
they come from."

Samantha wiped her eyes surreptitiously with the dishcloth and turned a scarlet face away from the window. Timothy was getting his "passle o' chips." Gay had spied him, and toddling over to his side, holding her dress above the prettiest little pair of feet that ever trod clover, had sat down on him (a favorite pastime of hers), and after jolting her fat little person up and down on his patient head, rolled herself over and gave him a series of bear-hugs. Timothy looked pale and languid, Samantha thought, and though Gay waited for a frolic with her most adorable smile, he only lifted her coral necklace to kiss the place where it hung, and tied on her sun-bonnet soberly. Samantha wished that Vilda had been looking out of the window. Her own heart did n't need softening, but somebody else's did, she was afraid.

"I 'm much obliged to you for takin' so much interest in the children," said Miss Vilda primly, " and partic'lerly for clearin' our characters, which everybody that lives in this village has to do for each other 'bout once a week, and the rest o' the time they take for spoilin' of 'em. And the Doctor's wife is very kind, but I should n't think o' sendin' the baby away so sudden while the boy is still here. It would n't be no kindness to Mis' Mayo, for she 'd have a reg'lar French and Indian war right on her premises. It was here the children came, just as you say, and it 's our duty to see 'em settled in good homes, but I shall take a few days more to think 'bout it, and I 'll let her know by Saturday night what we 've decided to do. — That 's the most meddlesome, inteferin', gossipin' woman in this county," she added, as Mrs. Silas Tarbox closed the front gate, " and I would n't have her do another day's work at this house if I did n't have to. But it 's worse for them that don't have her than for them that does. — Now there 's the Baptist minister drivin' up to the barn. What under the canopy does he want? Tell him Jabe ain't to home, Samanthy. No, you need n't, for he 's hitched, and seems to be comin' to the front door."

"I never could abide the looks of him," said Samantha, peering over Miss Vilda's shoulder. " No man with a light chiny blue eye like that oughter be allowed to go int' the ministry; for you can't love your brother whom you hev seen with that kind of an eye, and how are you goin' to love the Lord whom you hev not seen?"

Mr. Southwick, who was a spare little man in a long linen duster that looked as if it had not been in the water as often as its wearer, sat down timidly on the settle and cleared his throat.

" I 've come to talk with you on a little matter of business, Miss Cummins. Brother Slocum has — a — conferred with me on the subject of a — a — couple of unfortunate children who have — a — strayed, as it were, under your hospitable roof, and whom — a — you are properly anxious to place — a — under other rooves, as it were. Now you are aware, perhaps, that Mrs. Southwick and I have no children living, though we have at times had our quivers full of them — a — as the Scripture says ; but the Lord gave and the Lord hath taken away. Blessed be the name of the Lord, however, that is — a — neither here nor there. Brother Slocum has so interested us that my wife (who is leading the Woman's Auxiliary Praying Legion this afternoon or she would have come herself) wishes me to say that she would like to receive one of these — a — little waifs into our family on probation, as it were, and if satisfactory to both parties, to bring it up — a — somewhat as our own, in the nurture and admonition of the Lord."

Samantha waited, in breathless suspense.
Miss Vilda never would fling away an oppor-
tunity of putting a nameless, homeless child
under the roof of a minister of the Gospel,
even if he was a Baptist, with a chiny blue
eye.

At this exciting juncture there was a clatter of small feet; the door burst open, and
the "unfortunate waifs" under consideration raced across the floor to the table where
Miss Vilda and Samantha were seated.
Gay's sun-bonnet trailed behind her, every
hair on her head curled separately, and she
held her rag-doll upside down with entire
absence of decorum. Timothy's paleness,
whatever the cause, had disappeared for the
moment, and his eyes shone like stars.

"Oh, Miss Vilda!" he cried breathlessly;
"dear Miss Vilda and Samanthy, the gray
hen did want to have chickens, and that is
what made her so cross, and she is setting,
and we've found her nest in the alder
bushes by the pond!"

("G'ay hen's net in er buttes by er
pond," sung Gay, like a Greek chorus.)

"And we sat down softly beside the pond,
but Gay sat into it."

("Gay sat wite into it, an' dolly dot her

dess wet, but Gay nite ittle dirl; Gay did n't det wet!")

"And by and by the gray hen got off to get a drink of water" —

("To det a dink o' water" —)

"And we counted the eggs, and there were thirteen big ones!"

("Fir-teen drate bid ones!")

"So that the darling thing had to s-w-ell out to cover them up!"

("Darlin' fin ser-welled out an' tuvvered 'em up!") said Gay, going through the same operation.

"Yes," said Miss Vilda, looking covertly at Mr. Southwick (who had an eye for beauty, notwithstanding Samantha's strictures), "that's very nice, but you must n't stay here now; we are talkin' to the minister. Run away, both of you, and let the settin' hen alone. — Well, as I was goin' to say, Mr. Southwick, you 're very kind and so 's your wife, and I 'm sure Timothy, that 's the boy's name, would be a great help and comfort to both of you, if you 're fond of children, and we should be glad to have him near by, for we feel kind of responsible for him, though he 's no relation of ours. And we 'll think about the matter over night, and let you know in the morning."

" Yes, exactly, I see, I see ; but it was the young child, the — a — female child, that my wife desired to take into her family. She does not care for boys, and she is particularly fond of girls, and so am I, very fond of girls — a — in reason."

Miss Vilda all at once made up her mind on one point, and only wished that Samantha would n't stare at her as if she had never seen her before. " I 'm sorry to disappoint your wife, Mr. Southwick. It seems that Mrs. Tarbox and Jabez Slocum have been offerin' the child to every family in the village, and I s'pose bime bye they 'll have the politeness to offer her to me; but, at any rate, whether they do or not, I propose to keep her myself, and I 'd thank you to tell folks so, if they ask you. Mebbe you 'd better give it out from the pulpit, though I can let Mis' Tarbox know, and that will answer the same purpose. This is the place the baby was brought, and this is the place she 's goin' to stay."

" Vildy, you 're a good woman ! " cried Samantha, when the door closed on the Reverend Mr. Southwick. " I 'm proud o' you, Vildy, 'n' I take back all the hard thoughts I 've ben hevin' about you lately. The idee o' that chiny-eyed preacher thinkin' he was goin' to carry that child home in his buggy with hardly so much as sayin' ' Thank you, marm !' I like his Baptist imperdence ! His wife hed better wash his duster afore she adopts any children. If they 'd carry their theories 'bout immersion 's fur as their close, 't would n't be no harm."

" I don' know as I 'd have agreed to keep either of 'em ef the whole village had n't intefered and wanted to manage my business for me, and be so dretful charitable all of a sudden, and dictate to me and try to show me my duty. I have n't had a minute's peace for more 'n a fortnight, and now I hope they 'll let me alone. I 'll take the boy to the city to-morrow, if I live to see the light, and when I come back I 'll tie up the gate and keep the neighbors out till this nine days' wonder gets crowded out o' their heads by somethin' new."

" You 're goin' to take Timothy to the city, are you ? " asked Samantha sharply.

" That 's what I 'm goin' to do ; and the sooner the better for everybody concerned. Timothy, shut that door and run out to the barn, and don't you let me see you again till supper-time ; do you hear me ? "

" And you 're goin' to put him in one o' them Homes ? "

" Yes, I am. You see for yourself we can't find any place fer him hereabouts."

" Well, I 've ben waitin' for days to see what you was goin' to do, and now I 'll tell you what I 'm goin' to do, if you 'd like to know. I 'm goin' to keep Timothy myself ; to have and to hold from this time forth and for evermore, as the Bible says. That 's what I 'm goin' to do ! "

Miss Cummins gasped with astonishment.

" I mean what I say, Vildy. I ain't so well off as some, but I ain't a pauper, not by no means. I 've ben layin' by a little every year for twenty years, 'n' you know well enough what for ; but that 's all over for ever and ever, amen, thanks be ! And I ain't got chick nor child, nor blood relation in the world, and if I choose to take somebody to do for, why, it 's nobody's affairs but my own."

" You can't do it, and you sha'n't do it ! " said Miss Vilda excitedly. " You ain't goin' to make a fool of yourself, if I can help it. We can't have two children clutterin' up this place and eatin' us out of house and home, and that 's the end of it."

"It ain't the end of it, Vildy Cummins, not by no manner o' means! If we can't keep both of 'em, do you know what I think 'bout it? I think we'd ought to give away the one that everybody wants and keep the other that nobody does want, more fools they! That's religion, accordin' to my way o' thinkin'. I love the baby, dear knows; but see here. Who planned this thing all out? Timothy. Who took that baby up in his own arms and fetched her out o' that den o' thieves? Timothy. Who stood all the resk of gittin' that innocent lamb out o' that sink of iniquity, and hed wit enough to bring her to a place where she could grow up respectable? Timothy. And do you ketch him sayin' a word 'bout himself from fust to last? Not by no manner o' means. That ain't Timothy. And what doos the lovin' gen'rous, faithful little soul git? He gits his labor for his pains. He hears folks say right to his face that nobody wants him and everybody wants Gay. And if he did n't have a disposition like a cherubim-an-seraphim (and better, too, for they 'continually do cry,' now I come to think of it), he 'd be sour and bitter, 'stid o' bein' good as an angel in a picture-book from sun-up to sun-down!"

Miss Vilda was crushed by the overpowering weight of this argument, and did not even try to stem the resistless tide of Samantha's eloquence.

"And now folks is all of a high to take in the baby for a spell, jest for a plaything, because her hair curls, 'n' she 's han'some, 'n' light complected, 'n' cunning, 'n' a girl (whatever that amounts to is more 'n I know!), and that blessed boy is tread under foot as if he warn't no better 'n an angle-worm! And do you mean to tell me you don't see the Lord's hand in this hull bus'-ness, Vildy Cummins? There 's other kinds o' meracles besides buddin' rods 'n' burnin' bushes 'n' loaves 'n' fishes. What do you s'pose guided that boy to pass all the other houses in this village 'n' turn in at the White Farm? Don't you s'pose he was led? Well, I don't need a Bible nor yit a concordance to tell *me* he was. *He* did n't know there was plenty 'n' to spare inside this gate; a great, empty house 'n' full cellar, 'n' hay 'n' stock in the barn, and cow-pons in the bank, 'n' two lone, mis'able wo-men inside, with nothin' to do but keep flies out in summer-time, 'n' pile wood on in win-ter-time, till they got so withered up 'n'

gnarly they warn't hardly wuth getherin'
int' the everlastin' harvest! *He* did n't
know it, I say, but the Lord did; 'n' the
Lord's intention was to give us a chance to
make our callin' 'n' election sure, 'n' we
can't do that by turnin' our backs on His
messenger, and puttin' of him ou'doors!
The Lord intended them children should
stay together or He would n't 'a' started 'em
out that way; now that's as plain as the
nose on my face, 'n' that's consid'able plain
as I've ben told afore now, 'n' can see for
myself in the glass without any help from
anybody, thanks be!"

"Everybody'll laugh at us for a couple o'
soft-hearted fools," said Miss Vilda feebly,
after a long pause. "We'll be a spectacle
for the whole village."

"What if we be? Let's be a spectacle,
then!" said Samantha stoutly. "We'll be
a spectacle for the angels as well as the village, when you come to that! When they
look down 'n' see us gittin' outside this dooryard 'n' doin' one o' the Lord's chores for
the first time in ten or fifteen years, I guess
they'll be consid'able excited! But there's
no use in talkin', I've made up my mind,
Vildy. We've lived together for thirty

years 'n' ain't hardly hed an ugly word ('n'
dretful dull it hez ben for both of us!), 'n'
I sha'n't live nowheres else without you tell
me to go; but I've got lots o' good work in
me yit, 'n' I'm goin' to take that boy up 'n'
give him a chance, 'n' let him stay alongside o' the thing he loves best in the world.
And if there ain't room for all of us in the
fourteen rooms o' this part o' the house,
Timothy 'n' I can live in the L, as you've
allers intended I should if I got married.
And I guess this is 'bout as near to gittin'
married as either of us ever 'll git now, 'n'
consid'able nearer 'n I've expected to git,
lately. And I'll tell Timothy this very
night, when he goes to bed, for he's grievin'
himself into a fit o' sickness, as anybody can
tell that's got a glass eye in their heads!"

SCENE XIV.

A Point of Honor.

TIMOTHY JESSUP RUNS AWAY A SECOND TIME,
AND, LIKE OTHER BLESSINGS, BRIGHTENS AS
HE TAKES HIS FLIGHT.

It was almost dusk, and Jabe Slocum was
struggling with the nightly problem of getting the cow from the pasture without any
expenditure of personal effort. Timothy
was nowhere to be found, or he would go
and be glad to do the trifling service for
his kind friend without other remuneration
than a cordial "Thank you." Failing Timothy there was always Billy Pennell, who
would not go for a "Thank you," being a
boy of a sordid and miserly manner of
thought, but who would go for a cent and
chalk the cent up, which made it a more
reasonable charge than would appear to the
casual observer. So Jabe lighted his corn-
cob pipe, and extended himself under a wil-
low-tree beside the pond, singing in a cheerful fashion, —

"'Tremblin' sinner, calm your fears!
    Jesus is always ready.
Cease your sin and dry your tears,
    Jesus is always ready!'"

"And dretful lucky for you He is!" muttered Samantha, who had come to look for Timothy. "Jabe! Jabe! Has Timothy gone for the cow?"

"Dunno. Jest what I was goin' to ask you when I got roun' to it."

"Well, how are you goin' to find out?"

"Find out by seein' the cow if he hez gone, an' by not seein' no cow if he hain't. I'm comf'table either way it turns out. One o' them writin' fellers that was up here summerin' said, 'They also serve who'd ruther stan' 'n' wait''d be a good motto for me, 'n' he's about right when I've ben hayin'. Look down there at the shiners, ain't they cool? Gorry! I wish I was a fish!"

"If you was you wouldn't wear your fins out, that's certain!"

"Come now, Samanthy, don't be hard on a feller after his day's work. Want me to git up 'n' blow the horn for the boy?"

"No, thank you," answered Samantha cuttingly. "I wouldn't ask you to spend your precious breath for fear you'd be too

lazy to draw it in agin. When I want to
get anything done I can gen'ally spunk up
sprawl enough to do it myself, thanks be!"

"Wall now, Samanthy, you cheat the men-
folks out of a heap o' pleasure bein' so all-
fired independent, did ye know it?

"'Tremblin' sinner, calm your fears!
Jesus is always ready.'"

"When 'd you see him last?"

"I hain't seen him sence 'bout noon-time.
Warn't he into supper?"

"No. We thought he was off with you.
Well, I guess he's gone for the cow, but I
should think he'd be hungry. It's kind
o' queer."

Miss Vilda was seated at the open window in the kitchen, and Lady Gay was enthroned in her lap, sleepy, affectionate, tract-
able, adorable.

"How would you like to live here at the
White Farm, deary?" asked Miss Vilda.

"O, yet. I yike to live here if Timfy
doin' to live here too. I yike oo, I yike
Samfy, I yike Dabe, I yike white tat 'n'
white tow 'n' white bossy 'n' my boofely
desses 'n' my boofely dolly 'n' er day hen
'n' I yikes evelybuddy!"

"But you'd stay here like a nice little

girl if Timothy had to go away, would n't
you ? "

" No, I won't tay like nite ittle dirl if
Timfy do 'way. If Timfy do 'way, I do too.
I 's Timfy's dirl."

" But you 're too little to go away with
Timothy."

" Ven I ky an keam an kick an hold my
bwef — I s'ow you how ! "

" No, you need n't show me how," said
Vilda hastily. " Who do you love best,
deary, Samanthy or me ? "

" I yuv Timfy bet. Lemme twy rit-man-
poor-man-bedder-man-fief on your buckalins,
pease."

" Then you 'll stay here and be my little
girl, will you ? "

" Yet, I tay here an' be Timfy's ittle dirl.
Now oo p'ay by your own seff ittle while,
Mit Vildy, pease, coz I dot to det down an
find Samfy an' put my dolly to 'bed coz
she 's defful seepy."

" It 's half past eight," said Samantha
coming into the kitchen, " and Timothy ain't
nowheres to be found, and Jabe hain't seen
him sence noon-time."

" You need n't be scared for fear you 've
lost your bargain," remarked Miss Vilda

sarcastically. "There ain't so many places
open to the boy that he 'll turn his back on
this one, I guess!"

Yet, though the days of chivalry were
over, that was precisely what Timothy Jessup had done.

Wilkins's Wood was a quiet stretch of
timber land that lay along the banks of
Pleasant River; and though the natives (for
the most part) never noticed but that it was
paved with asphalt and roofed in with oil-
cloth, yet it was, nevertheless, the most
tranquil bit of loveliness in all the country
round. For there the river twisted and
turned and sparkled in the sun, and "bent
itself in graceful courtesies of farewell" to
the hills it was leaving; and kissed the vel-
vet meadows that stooped to drink from its
brimming cup; and lapped the trees gently,
as they hung over its crystal mirrors the
better to see their own fresh beauty. And
here it wound "about and in and out,"
laughing in the morning sunlight, to think
of the tiny streamlet out of which it grew;
paling and shimmering at evening when it
held the stars and moonbeams in its bosom;
and trembling in the night wind to think of

the great unknown sea into whose arms it was hurrying.

Here was a quiet pool where the rushes bent to the breeze and the quail dipped her wing; and there a winding path where the cattle came down to the edge, and having looked upon the scene and found it all very good, dipped their sleek heads to drink and drink and drink of the river's nectar. Here the first pink mayflowers pushed their sweet heads through the reluctant earth, and waxen Indian pipes grew in the moist places, and yellow violets hid themselves beneath their modest leaves.

And here sat Timothy, with all his heart in his eyes, bidding good-by to all this soft and tender loveliness. And there, by his side, faithful unto death (but very much in hopes of something better), sat Rags, and thought it a fine enough prospect, but one that could be beaten at all points by a bit of shed-view he knew of, — a superincumbent hash-pan, an empty milk-dish, and an ema-ciated white cat flying round a corner! The remembrance of these past joys brought the tears to his eyes, but he forbore to let them flow lest he should add to the griefs of his little master, which, for aught he knew, might be as heavy as his own.

Timothy was comporting himself, at this trying crisis, neither as a hero nor as a martyr. There is no need of exaggerating his virtues. Enough to say, not that he was a hero, but that he had in him the stuff out of which heroes are made. Win his heart and fire his imagination, and there is no splendid deed of which the little hero would not have been capable. But that he knew precisely what he was leaving behind, or what he was going forth to meet, would be saying too much. One thing he did know: that Miss Vilda had said distinctly that two was one too many, and that he was the objectionable unit referred to. And in addition to this he had more than once heard that very day that nobody in Pleasant River wanted him, but that there would be plenty of homes open to Gay if he were safely out of the way. A little allusion to a Home, which he caught when he was just bringing in a four-leafed clover to show to Samantha, completed the stock of ideas from which he reasoned. He was very clear on one point, and that was that he would never be taken alive and put in a Home with a capital H. He respected Homes, he approved of them, for other boys, but personally they were unpleasant to him, and he had no intention of dwelling in one if he could help it. The situation did not appear utterly hopeless in his eyes. He had his original dollar and eighty-five cents in money; Rags and he had supped like kings off wild blackberries and hard gingerbread; and, more than all, he was young and mercifully blind to all but the immediate present. Yet even in taking the most commonplace possible view of his character it would be folly to affirm that he was anything but unhappy. His soul was not sustained by the consciousness of having done a self-forgetting and manly act, for he was not old enough to have such a consciousness, which is something the good God gives us a little later on, to help us over some of the hard places.

"Nobody wants me! Nobody wants me!" he sighed, as he lay down under the trees. "Nobody ever did want me, — I wonder why! And everybody loves my darling Gay and wants to keep her, and I don't wonder about that. But, oh, if I only belonged to somebody! (Cuddle up close, little Ragsy; we've got nobody but just each other, and you can put your head into the other pocket that hasn't got the

gingerbread in it, if you please!) If I only
was like that little butcher's boy that he lets
ride on the seat with him, and hold the reins
when he takes meat into the houses, — or if
I only was that freckled-face boy with the
straw hat that lives on the way to the store!
His mother keeps coming out to the gate
on purpose to kiss him. Or if I was even
Billy Pennell! He's had three mothers
and two fathers in three years, Jabe says.
Jabe likes me, I think, but he can't have me
live at his house, because his mother is the
kind that needs plenty of room, he says, —
and Samanthy has no house. But I did
what I tried to do. I got away from Minerva Court and found a lovely place for
Gay to live, with two mothers instead of
one; and maybe they'll tell her about me
when she grows bigger, and then she'll know
I didn't want to run away from her, but
whether they tell her or not, she's only a
little baby, and boys must always take care
of girls; that's what my dream - mother
whispers to me in the night, — and that's
. . . what . . . I'm always . . ."

Come! gentle sleep, and take this friendless little knight-errant in thy kind arms!
Bear him across the rainbow bridge, and lull

him to rest with the soft plash of waves and sighing of branches! Cover him with thy mantle of dreams, sweet goddess, and give him in sleep what he hath never had in waking!

Meanwhile, a more dramatic scene was being enacted at the White Farm. It was nine o'clock, and Samantha had gone from pond to garden, shed to barn, and gate to dairy, a dozen times, but there was no sign of Timothy. Gay had refused to be undressed till "Timfy" appeared on the premises, but had fallen asleep in spite of the most valiant resolution, and was borne upstairs by Samantha, who made her ready for bed without waking her.

As she picked up the heap of clothes to lay them neatly on a chair, a bit of folded paper fell from the bosom of the little dress. She glanced at it, turned it over and over, read it quite through. Then, after retiring behind her apron a moment, she went swiftly downstairs to the dining-room where Miss Avilda and Jabe were sitting.

"There!" she exclaimed, with a triumphant sob, as she laid the paper down in front of the astonished couple. "That's a letter from Timothy. He's run away, 'n' I don't blame him a mite 'n' I hope folks 'll be satisfied now they've got red of the blessed angel, 'n' turned him ou'doors without a roof to his head! Read it out, 'n' see what kind of a boy we've showed the door to!"

Dere Miss vilder and sermanthy. i herd you say i cood not stay here enny longer and other peeple sed nobuddy wood have me and what you sed about the home but as i do not like homes i am going to run away if its all the same to you. Please give Jabe back his birds egs with my love and i am sorry i broak the humming-bird's one but it was a naxident. Pleas take good care of gay and i will come back and get her when I am ritch. I thank you very mutch for such a happy time and the white farm is the most butifull plase in the whole whirld.　　　　　　　　　　Tim.

p. s. i wood not tell you if i was going to stay but billy penel thros stones at the white cow witch i fere will get into her milk so no more from　　　　　Tim.

i am sorry not to say good by but i am afrade on acount of the home so i put them here.

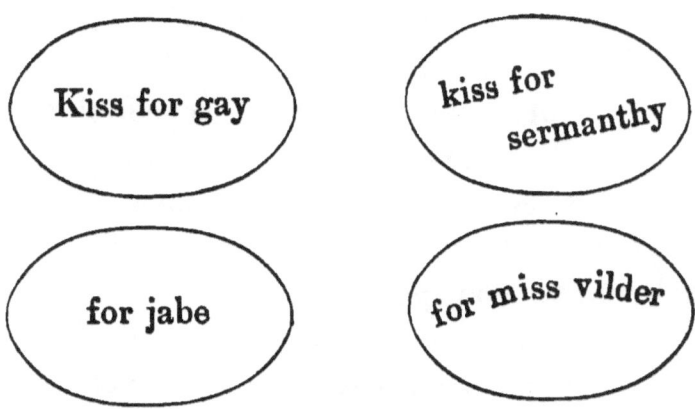

Kiss for gay

kiss for
sermanthy

for jabe

for miss vilder

The paper fell from Miss Vilda's trembling fingers, and two salt tears dropped into the kissing places.

"The Lord forgive me!" she said at length (and it was many a year since any one had seen her so moved). "The Lord forgive me for a hard-hearted old woman, and give me a chance to make it right. Not one reproachful word does he say to us about showin' partiality, — not one! And my heart has kind of yearned over that boy from the first, but just because he had Marthy's eyes he kept bringin' up the past to me, and I never looked at him without rememberin' how hard and unforgivin' I'd

ben to her, and thinkin' if I'd petted and
humored her a little and made life pleasanter,
perhaps she'd never have gone away. And
I've scrimped and saved and laid up money
till it comes hard to pay it out, and when I
thought of bringin' up and schoolin' two
children I cal'lated I could n't afford it; and
yet I've got ten thousand dollars in the
bank and the best farm for miles around.
Samanthy, you go fetch my bonnet and
shawl, — Jabe, you go and hitch up Maria,
and we'll go after that boy and fetch him
back if he's to be found anywheres above
ground! And if we come across any more
o' the same family trampin' around the
country, we'll bring them along home while
we're about it, and see if we can't get
some sleep and some comfort out o' life.
And the Missionary Society can look somewheres else for money. There's plenty o'
folks that don't get good works set right
down in their front yards for 'em to do.
I'll look out for the individyals for a spell,
and let the other folks support the societies!"

SCENE XV.

Wilkins's Woods.

LIKE ALL DOGS IN FICTION THE FAITHFUL RAGS
GUIDES MISS VILDA TO HIS LITTLE MASTER.

SAMANTHA ran out to the barn to hold the
lantern and see that Jabe did n't go to sleep
while he was harnessing Maria. But he
seemed unusually "spry" for him, although
he was conducting himself in a somewhat
strange and unusual manner. His loose figure shook from time to time, as with severe
chills; he seemed too weak to hold up the
shafts, and so he finally dropped them and
hung round Maria's neck in a sort of mild,
speechless convulsion.

"What under the canopy ails you, Jabe
Slocum?" asked Samantha. "I s'pose it 's
one o' them everlastin' old addled jokes o'
yourn you 're tryin' to hatch out, but it 's a
poor time to be jokin' now. What 's the
matter with you?"

"'Ask me no questions 'n' I 'll tell you no
lies,' is an awful good motto," chuckled Jabe,

with a new explosion of mirth that stretched his mouth to an alarming extent. "Oh, there, I can't hold in 'nother minute. I shall bust if I don' tell somebody! Set down on that nail kag, Samanthy, 'n' I'll let you hev a leetle slice o' this joke — if you'll keep it to yourself. You see I know — 'bout — whar — to look — for this here — runaway!"

"You hev n't got him stowed away anywheres, hev you? If you hev, it'll be the last joke you'll play on Vildy Cummins, I can tell you that much, Jabe Slocum."

"No, I hain't stowed him away, but I can tell putty nigh whar he's stowed · hisself away, and I'm ready to die a-laffin' to see how it's all turned out jest as I suspicioned 't would. You see, Samanthy Ann, I thought 'bout a week ago 't would be well enough to kind·o' create a demand for the young ones so 't they'd hev some kind of a market value, and so I got Elder Southwick 'n' Aunt Hitty kind o' started on that tack, 'n' it worked out slick as a whistle, tho' they did n't know I was usin' of 'em as innercent instruments, and Aunt Hitty don't need much encouragement to talk; it's a heap easier for her to drizzle 'n it is to hold up! Well, I've ben surmisin' for a week that the boy meant to run away, and

to-day I was dead sure of it; for he come to
me this afternoon, when I was restin' a spell
on account o' the hot sun, and he was awful
low-sperrited, 'n' he asked me every nam-
able kind of a question you ever hearn tell
of, and all so simple-minded that I jest
turned him inside out 'thout his knowin'
what I was doin'. Well, when I found out
what he was up to I could 'a' stopped him
then 'n' there, tho' I don' know 's I would
anyhow, for I should n't like livin' in a 'sylum any better 'n he doos; but thinks I to
myself, thinks I, I 'd better let him run
away, jest as he 's a plannin', — and why?
Cause it 'll show what kind o' stuff he 's made
of, and that he ain't no beggar layin' roun'
whar he ain't wanted, but a self-respectin'
boy that 's wuth lookin' after. And thinks I,
Samanthy, 'n' I know the wuth of him a'-
ready, but there 's them that hain't waked up
to it yit, namely, Miss Vildy Trypheny Cummins; and as Miss Vildy Trypheny Cummins
is that kind o' cattle that can't be drove,
but hez to be kind o' coaxed along, mebbe
this runnin'-away bizness 'll be the thing
that 'll fetch her roun' to our way o' thinkin'. Now I would n't deceive nobody for a
farm down East with a pig on it, but thinks

I, there ain't no deceivin' 'bout this. He don' know I know he's goin' to run away, so he's all square; and he never told me nothin' 'bout his plans, so I'm all square; and Miss Vildy's good as eighteen-karat gold when she gets roun' to it, so she'll be all square; and Samanthy's got her blinders on 'n' don't see nothin' to the right nor to the left, so she's all square. And I ain't infeterin' with nobody. I'm jest lettin' things go the way they've started, 'n' stan'in' to one side to see whar they'll fetch up, kind o' like Providence. I'm leavin' Miss Vildy a free agent, but I'm shapin' circumstances so's to give her a chance. But, land! if I'd fixed up the thing to suit myself I could n't 'a' managed it as Timothy hez, 'thout knowin' that he was managin' anything. Look at that letter bizness now! I could n't 'a' writ that letter better myself! And the sperrit o' the little feller, jest takin' his dorg 'n' lightin' out with nothin' but a perlite good-bye! Well I can't stop to talk no more 'bout it now, or we won't ketch him, but we'll jest try Wilkins's Woods, Maria, 'n' see how that goes. The river road leads to Edgewood 'n' Hillside, whar there's consid'able hayin' bein' done, as I happened to mention to Timo-

thy this afternoon; and plenty o' blackberries
'side the road, 'specially after you pass the
wood-pile on the left-hand side, whar there's
a reg'lar garding of 'em right 'side of an old
hoss-blanket that's layin' there; one that I
happened to leave there one time when I
was sleepin' ou'doors for my health, and
that was this afternoon 'bout five o'clock, so
I guess it hain't changed its location sence."

Jabe and Miss Vilda drove in silence
along the river road that skirted Wilkins's
Woods, a place where Jabe had taken Timothy more than once, so he informed Miss
Vilda, and a likely road for him to travel if
he were on his way to some of the near villages.

Poor Miss Vilda! Fifty years old, and
in twenty summers and winters scarcely one
lovely thought had blossomed into lovelier
deed and shed its sweetness over her arid
and colorless life. And now, under the
magic spell of tender little hands and innocent lips, of luminous eyes that looked wist-
fully into hers for a welcome, and the touch
of a groping helplessness that fastened upon
her strength, the woman in her woke into
life, and the beauty and fragrance of long-
ago summers came back again as in a dream.

After having driven three or four miles, they heard a melancholy sound in the distance; and as they approached a huge wood-pile on the left side of the road, they saw a small woolly form perched on a little rise of ground, howling most melodiously at the August moon, that hung like a ball of red fire in the cloudless sky.

"That's a sign of death in the family, ain't it, Jabe?" whispered Miss Vilda faintly.

"So they say," he answered cheerfully; "but if 't is, I can 'count for it, bein' as how I fertilized the pond lilies with a mess o' four white kittens this afternoon; and as Rags was with me when I done it, he may know what he's bayin' 'bout, — if 't is Rags, 'n' it looks enough like him to be him, — 'n' it is him, by Jiminy, 'n' Timothy's sure to be somewheres near. I'll get out 'n' look roun' a little."

"You set right still, Jabe, I'll get out myself, for if I find that boy I've got something to say to him that nobody can say for me."

As Jabe drew the wagon up beside the fence, Rags bounded out to meet them. He knew Maria, bless your soul, the minute he clapped his eyes on her, and as he approached Miss Vilda's congress boot his quivering whiskers seemed to say, " Now, where have I smelled that boot before? If I mistake not, it has been applied to me more than once. Ha! I have it! Miss Vilda Cummins of the White Farm, owner of the white cat and hash-pan, and companion of the lady with the firm hand, who wields the broom!" whereupon he leaped up on Miss Cummins's black alpaca skirts, and made for her flannel garters in a way that she particularly disliked.

" Now," said she, " if he's anything like the dogs you hear tell of, he'll take us right to Timothy."

" Wall, I don' know," said Jabe cautiously; " there's so many kinds o' dorg in him you can't hardly tell what he will do. When dorgs is mixed beyond a certain p'int it kind o' muddles up their instincks, 'n' you can't rely on 'em. Still you might try him. Hold still, 'n' see what he'll do."

Miss Vilda " held still," and Rags jumped on her skirts.

" Now, set down, 'n' see whar he'll go."

Miss Vilda sat down, and Rags went into her lap.

"Now, make believe start somewheres, 'n' mebbe he 'll get ahead 'n' put you on the right track."

Miss Vilda did as she was told, and Rags followed close at her heels.

"Gorry! I never see sech a fool! — or wait, — I 'll tell you. what 's the matter with him. Mebbe he ain't sech a fool as he looks. You see, he knows Timothy wants to run away and don't want to be found 'n' clapped into a 'sylum, 'n' nuther does he. And not bein' sure o' your intentions, he ain't a-goin' to give hisself away; that 's the way I size Mr. Rags up!"

"Nice doggy, nice doggy!" shuddered Miss Vilda, as Rags precipitated himself upon her again. "Show me where Timothy is, and then we 'll go back home and have some nice bones. Run and find your little master, that 's a good doggy!"

It would be a clever philosopher who could divine Rags's special method of logic, or who could write him down either as fool or sage. Suffice it to say that, at this moment (having run in all other possible directions, and wishing, doubtless, to keep on moving), he ran round the wood-pile; and Miss Vilda, following close behind, came

upon a little figure stretched on a bit of gray
blanket. The pale face shone paler in the
moonlight; there were traces of tears on the
cheeks; but there was a heavenly smile on
his parted lips, as if his dream-mother had
rocked him to sleep in her arms. Rags stole
away to Jabe (for even mixed dogs have
some delicacy), and Miss Vilda went down
on her knees beside the sleeping boy.

"Timothy, Timothy, wake up!"

No answer.

"Timothy, wake up! I've come to take
you home!"

Timothy woke with a sob and a start at
that hated word, and seeing Miss Vilda at
once jumped to conclusions.

"Please, please, dear Miss Vildy, don't
take me to the Home, but find me some
other place, and I'll never, never run away
from it!"

"My blessed little boy, I've come to take
you back to your own home at the White
Farm."

It was too good to believe all at once.
"Nobody wants me there," he said hesitat-
ingly.

"Everybody wants you there," replied
Miss Vilda, with a softer note in her voice

than anybody had ever heard there before.
"Samantha wants you, Gay wants you, and
Jabe is waiting out here with Maria, for he
wants you."

"But do you want me?" faltered the
boy.

"I want you more than all of 'em put together, Timothy; I want you, and I need
you most of all," cried Miss Vilda, with the
tears coursing down her withered cheeks;
"and if you'll only forgive me for hurtin'
your feelin's and makin' you run away, you
shall come to the White Farm and be my
own boy as long as you live."

"Oh, Miss Vildy, darling Miss Vildy!
are we both of us adopted, and are we truly
going to live with you all the time and never
have to go to the Home?" Whereupon, the
boy flung his loving arms round Miss Vilda's neck in an ecstasy of gratitude; and in
that sweet embrace of trust and confidence
and joy, the stone was rolled away, once and
forever, from the sepulchre of Miss Vilda's
heart, and Easter morning broke there.

SCENE XVI.

The New Homestead.

TIMOTHY'S QUEST IS ENDED, AND SAMANTHA
SAYS " COME ALONG, DAVE ! "

"Jabe Slocum! Do you know it's goin'
on seven o'clock 'n' not a single chore
done?"

Jabe yawned, turned over, and listened to
Samantha's unwelcome voice, which (consid-
erably louder than the voice of conscience)
came from the outside world to disturb his
delicious morning slumbers.

"Jabe Slocum! Do you hear me?"

"Hear you? Gorry! you'd wake the
seven sleepers if they was any whar within
ear-shot!"

"Well, will you git up?"

"Yes, I'll git up if you're goin' to hev a
brash 'bout it, but I wish you hed n't waked
me so awful suddent. 'Don't ontwist the
mornin' glory''s my motto. Wait a spell 'n'
the sun 'll do it, 'n' save a heap o' wear 'n'
tear besides. Go 'long! I'll git up."

"I've heerd that story afore, 'n' I won't go 'long tell I hear you step foot on the floor."

"Scoot! I tell yer I'll be out in a jiffy."

"Yes, I think I see yer. Your jiffies are consid'able like golden opportunities, there ain't more 'n one of 'em in a lifetime!" and having shot this Parthian arrow Samantha departed, as one having done her duty in that humble sphere of action to which it had pleased Providence to call her.

These were beautiful autumn days at the White Farm. The orchards were gleaming, the grapes hung purple on the vines, and the odor of ripening fruit was in the hazy air. The pink spirea had cast its feathery petals by the gray stone walls, but the welcome golden-rod bloomed in royal profusion along the brown waysides, and a crimson leaf hung here and there in the treetops, just to give a hint of the fall styles in color. Heaps of yellow pumpkins and squashes lay in the corners of the fields; cornstalks bowed their heads beneath the weight of ripened ears; beans threatened to burst through their yellow pods; the sound of the threshing machine was heard in the land; and the "hull univarse wanted to be waited on to once," according to Jabe Slocum; for, as he affirmed, " Yer could n't ketch up with your work nohow, for if yer set up nights 'n' worked Sundays, the craps 'd ripen 'n' go to seed on yer 'fore yer could git 'em harvested ! "

And if there was peace and plenty without there was quite as much within doors.

" I can't hardly tell what 's the matter with me these days," said Samantha Ann to Miss Vilda, as they sat peeling and slicing apples for drying. " My heart has felt like a stun these last years, and now all to once it 's so soft I 'm ashamed of it. Seems to me there never was such a summer ! The hay never smelt so sweet, the birds never sang so well, the currants never jelled so hard ! Why I can't kick the cat, though she 's more everlastin'ly under foot 'n ever, 'n' pretty soon I sha'n't even have sprawl enough to jaw Jabe Slocum. I b'lieve it 's nothin' in the world but them children ! They keep a runnin' after me, 'n' it 's dear Samanthy here, 'n' dear Samanthy there, jest as if I warn't a hombly old maid; 'n' they take holt o' my hands on both sides o' me, 'n' won't stir a step tell I go to see the chickens with 'em, 'n' the pig, 'n' one thing 'n' 'nother, 'n' clappin' their hands

when I make 'em gingerbread men! And
that reminds me, I see the school-teacher
goin' down along this mornin,' 'n' I run out
to see how Timothy was gittin' along in his
studies. She says he 's the most ex-tra-ordi-
nary scholar in this deestrick. She says he
takes holt of every book she gives him jest
as if 't was reviewin' 'stid o' the first time
over. She says when he speaks pieces, Fri-
day afternoons, all the rest o' the young ones
set there with their jaws hangin,' 'n' some of
'em laughin' 'n' cryin' 't the same time. She
says we 'd oughter see some of his comp'si-
tions, 'n' she 'll show us some as soon as she
gits 'em back from her beau that works at
the Waterbury Watch Factory, and they 're
goin' to be married 's quick as she gits
money enough saved up to buy her weddin'
close; 'n' I told her not to put it off too long
or she 'd hev her close on her hands, 'stid of
her back. She says Timothy 's at the head
of the hull class, but, land! there ain't a boy
in it that knows enough to git his close on
right sid' out. She 's a splendid teacher,
Miss Boothby is! She tells me the seeleck
men hev raised her pay to four dollars a
week 'n' she to board herself, 'n' she 's wuth
every cent of it. I like to see folks well paid

that 's got the patience to set in doors 'n'
cram information inter young ones that don't
care no more 'bout learnin' 'n' a skunk-black-
bird. She give me Timothy's writin' book
for you to see what he writ in it yesterday,
'n' she hed to keep him in 't recess 'cause he
did n't copy 'Go to the ant thou sluggard and
be wise,' as he 'd oughter. Now let 's see what
't is. My grief! it 's poetry sure 's you 're
born. I can tell it in a minute 'cause it don't
come out to the aidge o' the book one side or
the other. Read it out loud, Vildy."

> " ' Oh ! the White Farm and the White Farm !
>   I love it with all my heart ;
>   And I 'm to live at the White Farm,
>   Till death it do us part.' "

Miss Vilda lifted her head, intoxicated
with the melody she had evoked. " Did you
ever hear anything like that," she exclaimed
proudly.

> " ' Oh ! the White Farm and the White Farm !
>   I love it with all my heart ;
>   And I 'm to live at the White Farm,
>   Till death it do us part.' "

" Just hear the sent'ment of it, and the
way it sings along like a tune. I 'm goin'
to show that to the minister this very night,
and that boy 's got to have the best educa-

tion there is to be had if we have to mort-
gage the farm."

Samantha Ann was right. The old homestead wore a new aspect these days, and a
love of all things seemed to have crept into
the hearts of its inmates, as if some beneficent fairy of a spider were spinning a web
of tenderness all about the house, or as if a
soft light had dawned in the midst of great
darkness and was gradually brightening
into the perfect day.

In the midst of this new-found gladness
and the sweet cares that grew and multiplied
as the busy days went on, Samantha's appetite for happiness grew by what it fed upon,
so that before long she was a little unhappy
that other people (some more than others)
were not as happy as she; and Aunt Hitty
was heard to say at the sewing-circle (which
had facilities for gathering and disseminat-
ing news infinitely superior to those of the
Associated Press), that Samantha Ann Ripley looked so péart and young this summer,
Dave Milliken had better spunk up and try
again.

But, alas! the younger and fresher and
happier Samantha looked, the older and
sadder and meeker David appeared, till all

hopes of his "spunking up" died out of the village heart; and, it might as well be stated, out of Samantha's also. She always thought about it at sundown, for it was at sundown that all their quarrels and reconciliations had taken place, inasmuch as it was the only leisure time for week-day courting at Pleasant River.

It was sundown now; Miss Vilda and Jabez Slocum had gone to Wednesday evening prayer-meeting, and Samantha was looking for Timothy to go to the store with her on some household errands. She had seen the children go into the garden a half hour before, Timothy walking gravely, with his book before him, Gay blowing over the grass like a feather, and so she walked towar's the summer-house.

Timothy was not there, but little Lady Gay was having a party all to herself, and the scene was such a pretty one that Samantha stooped behind the lattice and listened.

There was a table spread for four, with bits of broken china and shells for dishes, and pieces of apple and gingerbread for the feast. There were several dolls present (notably one without any head, who was not

likely to shine at a dinner party), but Gay's
first-born sat in her lap; and only a mother
could have gazed upon such a battered thing
and loved it. For Gay took her pleasures
madly, and this faithful creature had shared
them all; but not having inherited her mother's somewhat rare recuperative powers,
she was now fit only for a free bed in a
hospital, — a state of mind and body which
she did not in the least endeavor to conceal.
One of her shoe-button eyes dangled by a
linen thread in a blood-curdling sort of way;
her nose, which had been a pink glass bead,
was now a mere spot, ambiguously located.
Her red worsted lips were sadly raveled, but
that she did not regret, " for it was kissin'
as done it." Her yarn hair was attached
to her head with safety-pins, and her in-
ternal organs intruded themselves on the
public through a gaping wound in the side.
Never mind! if you have any curiosity to
measure the strength of the ideal, watch a
child with her oldest doll. Rags sat at the
head of the dinner-table, and had taken the
precaution to get the headless doll on his
right, with a view to eating her gingerbread
as well as his own, — doing no violence to
the proprieties in this way, but rather con-
cealing her defects from a carping public.

" I tell you sompfin' ittle Mit Vildy Tummins," Gay was saying to her battered off-
spring. " You's doin' to have a new ittle
sit-ter to-mowowday, if you's a dood ittle
dirl an does to seep nite an kick, you *ser-
weet* ittle Vildy Tummins! (All this punctu-
ated with ardent squeezes fraught with delicious agony to one who had a wound in her
side!) " Vay fink you's worn out, 'weety,
but we know you is n't, don' we, 'weety?
An I'll tell you nite ittle tory to-night,
tause you is n't seepy. Wunt there was a
ittle day hen 'at tole a net an' laid fir-teen
waw edds in it, an bime bye erleven or sev-
enteen ittle chits f'ew out of 'em, an Mit Vildy 'dopted 'em all! I n't that a nite tory,
you *ser-weet* ittle Mit Vildy Tummins? "

Samantha hardly knew why the tears
should spring to her eyes as she watched the
dinner party, — unless it was because we can
scarcely look at little children in their unconscious play without a sort of sadness,
partly of pity and partly of envy, and of
longing too, as for something lost and gone.
And Samantha could look back to the time
when she had sat at little tables set with
bits of broken china, yes, in this very summer-house, and little Martha was always so

gay, and David used to laugh so! "But there was no use in tryin' to make folks any dif'rent, 'specially if they was such nat'ral born fools they could n't see a hole in a grindstun 'thout hevin' it hung on their noses!" and with these large and charitable views of human nature, Samantha walked back to the gate, and met Timothy as he came out of the orchard. She knew then what he had been doing. The boy had certain quaint thoughts and ways that were at once a revelation and an inspiration to these two plain women, and one of them was this. To step softly into the side orchard on pleasant evenings, and without a word, before or afterwards, to lay a nosegay on Martha's little white doorplate. And if Miss Vilda chanced to be at the window he would give her a quiet little smile, as much as to say, "We have no need of words, we two!" And Vilda, like one of old, hid all these doings in her heart of hearts, and loved the boy with a love passing knowledge.

Samantha and Timothy walked down the hill to the store. Yes, David Milliken was sitting all alone on the loafer's bench at the door, and why was n't he at prayer-meetin' where he ought to be? She was glad she

chanced to have on her clean purple calico,
and that Timothy had insisted on putting a
pink Ma'thy Washington geranium in her
collar, for it was just as well to make folks'
mouth water whether they had sense enough
to eat or not.

"Who is that sorry-looking man that always sits on the bench at the store, Samanthy?"

"That's David Milliken."

"Why does he look so sorry, Samanthy?"

"Oh, he's all right. He likes it fust-
rate, wearin' out that hard bench settin' on
it night in 'n' night out, like a bump on a
log! But, there, Timothy, I've gone 'n'
forgot the whole pepper, 'n' we're goin' to
pickle seed cowcumbers to-morrer. You
take the lard home 'n' put it in the cold
room, 'n' ondress Gay 'n' git her to bed, for
I've got to call int' Mis' Mayhew's goin'
along back."

It was very vexatious to be obliged to pass
David Milliken a second time; "though
there warn't no sign that he cared anything
about it one way or 'nother, bein' blind as a
bat, 'n' deef as an adder, 'n' dumb as a fish,
'n' settin' stockstill there with no coat on,
'n' the wind blowin' up for rain, 'n' four o'

the Millikens layin' in the churchyard with gallopin' consumption." It was in this frame of mind that she purchased the whole pepper, which she could have eaten at that moment as calmly as if it had been marrow-fat peas; and in this frame of mind she might have continued to the end of time had it not been for one of those unconsidered trifles that move the world when the great forces have given up trying. As she came out of the store and passed David, her eye fell on a patch in the flannel shirt that covered his bent shoulders. The shirt was gray and (oh, the pity of it!) the patch was red; and it was laid forlornly on outside, and held by straggling stitches of carpet thread put on by patient, clumsy fingers. That patch had an irresistible pathos for a woman!

Samantha Ann Ripley never exactly knew what happened. Even the wisest of down-East virgins has emotional lapses once in a while, and she confessed afterwards that her heart riz right up inside of her like a yeast cake. Mr. Berry, the postmaster, was in the back of the store reading postal cards. Not a soul was in sight. She managed to get down over the steps, though something with

the strength of tarred ship-ropes was draw-
ing her back; and then, looking over her
shoulder with her whole brave, womanly
heart in her swimming eyes, she put out her
hand and said, " Come along, Dave ! "

And David straightway gat him up from
the loafer's bench and went unto Samantha
gladly.

And they remembered not past unhappi-
ness because of present joy; nor that the
chill of coming winter was in the air, because it was summer in their hearts: and
this is the eternal magic of love.